Books by Kathleen Pennell

Pony Investigator Series
The Case of the Missing Money
The Case of the Phantom Stallion
The Case of the Midnight Stranger
The Case of the Mysterious Circus
The Case of the Secret Passage
The Case of the Mirror Image

The Adventures In Time Series
The Door into Time
Rescued in Time

Lancelot Maddox Series
The Boy on the Bench
Ragtag Rescue
The Missing Agent
Plane Down

A Treadwell Mystery Series
The Face in the Water
The Man at the Ruins

LANCELOT MADDOX SERIES
BOOK 1

The boy on the bench
and other stories

KATHLEEN PENNELL

www.kathleenpennell.com

Table of Contents

The Boy on the Bench
Chapter 1

At exactly four fifteen, Lancelot would be offered a job at an intelligence agency. Until then, it was just an ordinary summer day.

Lancelot sneaked out the backdoor while his mother was in her office working. It depressed him that she always gave him two kisses and a hearty hug whenever he left the house. Lancelot's two older brothers, Gawain and Tristam, upheld the family tradition of soccer stardom, while Lancelot was a total nerd and destined to be the designated bench warmer that fall.

So, at three o'clock every day, he shouldered his backpack, hooked two mechanical pencils inside his shirt pocket, and walked to the park. By the time soccer begins, sitting on the bench will feel natural. It's not too bad really, because he solves complicated codes and puzzles inside his puzzle book while he practices being benched on the bench.

For two weeks, he'd sat undisturbed and unnoticed. Yet, as the town clock struck three-thirty, someone stopped on the sidewalk in front of him. He'd just figured out how to solve a puzzle listed in the 'difficult' category and was ready to put pencil to puzzle when a shadow began to snake its way across his page. He was really rather irritated. Glancing up, he saw a woman staring at him. She was the kind of woman so incredibly ordinary in appearance that if forced to give a description, the word 'average' would fill every box.

Except for his mother, Lancelot had never been the object of anyone's focus. He drew his brows together and repositioned his glasses on his nose. He'd never initiated a conversation in his entire life. "Why are you staring at me?" he asked.

The woman floated forward and slid down next to him. "I've just been given a gift."

Unwilling to relinquish his cherished spot in the middle of the bench, Lancelot merely leaned away from the woman.

"Aren't you going to ask me what it is?"

"I'd rather not."

"It's you."

Lancelot wasn't at all sure what she meant but found it rather puzzling.

"Now, don't be alarmed, but I'm going to pat your arm and smile, and I want you to smile back at me." The woman patted his arm and stretched her mouth forming an odd expression.

Lancelot hated being patted. That's what his brothers did at the end of every game. So, he deserted his cherished spot on the bench and scooted over where she was out of range. "Who are you, and why are you pretending to know me?"

The woman threw her head back and cackled, then dropped her voice, leaned in with another one of her odd expressions. "I may only have time to explain this once, so listen carefully. Some dangerous people are following me. Don't bother looking about the park because you won't see them."

"Are they trying to rob you?"

"You don't know the half of it. Look, if you'll just walk around the pond with me, I'll disappear from your life forever."

"Couldn't you disappear from my life forever while I stay here? I'm really rather busy at the moment."

The odd expression drooped a bit. "Look, kid, you're not doing anything right now, and I need about ten minutes of your entire life. Is that asking too much?"

In point of fact, Lancelot could indulge this persistent person for a few minutes with the promise that she'd 'disappear from his life forever'. He gathered his puzzles and carefully arranged them inside his backpack, then secured his mechanical pencils in his shirt pocket. Sliding his arm through the strap, he dragged his feet along the sidewalk and around the pond. The temptation to look over his shoulder was nearly irresistible. "What do these people want?"

The woman patted her purse.

Lancelot glanced with a certain amount of wonder at the stained straw bag with its missing handle. "They want that purse?"

"Of course, not," the woman hissed. "They want what's inside it."

"They want your money?"

"No! Stop asking questions."

As they trundled along, the woman drew her purse to the front and slid open the clasp. Reaching inside, she dug out a small piece of brown paper folded over several times and sealed with red wax. "I'm going to give this to you, but we can't allow them to see it. Do you understand what I mean?"

Once again, Lancelot resisted the overwhelming temptation to look over his shoulder. "Sure, I understand what you mean., but…"

"Don't ask," the woman hissed again. "Now, this is what I want you to do. Hold my hand for a moment and I'll slip this message to you." She looked down at Lancelot and waited.

Not once within given memory had Lancelot held hands with anyone, and now this. Gritting his teeth, he gave her the flat of his hand. After he wrapped his fingers around the small square, folder paper, he drew his hand away.

Lancelot lifted his hand to study it, but the woman said, "Don't look at it! You'll be safe as long as they think I still have it. Do you understand?"

Lancelot nearly choked. Was this woman totally insane or was there just a shred of truth in what she was saying? What was inside this wad of paper that was so important?

They'd nearly circled the pond, where Lancelot's commitment ended when the woman's fidgeting increased considerably. Growing tired of this ridiculous game, he extended the arm containing the paper. "I need to get back to work, so why don't you take this back."

"You call working on a few puzzles work?! Look, this is a matter of life and death! It's a matter of national security! Don't you get it?"

Lancelot gave it some thought then said, "No."

The woman grabbed his fist as though they were shaking hands. "Look, kid, you've got to deliver this to 434 Back Street," she said while her eyes bolted from side to side.

"I can't see anyone around here, so why can't you take this yourself?"

"You can't see air either, can you? But that doesn't mean it's not there, does it?"

"Air is invisible; people are not," Lancelot stated with the firm conviction of someone who thoroughly understood what was real and what wasn't.

The odd expression disappeared. "Look, take it to 434 Back Street and go home. I'm sure they'll follow me rather than you, because you're just a goofy looking kid, so you don't have to worry about being runover by a car or shot." Having said that, she fled through an alley and disappeared.

'Goofy looking kid'. Well, he'd been called worse. Lancelot's shoulders relaxed after he was free of the touchy-patty woman. "434 Back Street." The trash can was a tempting ten feet away, but the woman seemed rather desperate. Stuffing his hands inside his pockets, he trudged along, glancing up at intersections in case the woman was right, and someone might actually attempt to run him down.

Chapter 2

Within a few minutes, he reached the doorstep of his destination. It was a typical gray, nondescript building, except the door didn't possess a doorknob or handle.

"Yes?" came a sharp voice. Lancelot jumped and looked for a speaker. When he failed to respond, the voice added, "What is it?"

"I'm—I'm here to deliver a piece of paper," Lancelot said attempting to steady his voice.

There was a soft clicking sound and the door swung soundlessly open. Lancelot seriously considered pitching the small, sealed piece of paper through the door and returning to the safety of his bench. But the voice said. "Enter!"

As he stepped across the threshold, an older, slender, gray-haired man stepped out of an office. "What is it, kid?" he asked.

No one ever called Lancelot a kid. Now, within the span of twenty-minutes, it had happened several times and he wasn't at all sure he liked it. He swallowed as he looked down a long, dark hallway. Closed doors appeared every twelve feet. It was deathly quiet. He looked up at the man who was about four inches taller than he was. "Well, it's like this," he said. "This sort of odd-looking woman gave me this piece of paper and told me to bring it here. I haven't looked at it," he assured the unsmiling man extending his hand and opening his palm. "See. The red wax is still in place."

The man looked at Lancelot then at the brown folded paper with the red wax sealing it. His face revealed nothing, but there was a slight change in his brow. He lifted it ever so slightly. But Lancelot was the noticing kind and he saw it.

The man's eyes rose, and he studied the boy standing there. The kid had wavy, brown hair and greenish eyes set behind glasses. The nerdy rather than the athletic type. He recognized the brown paper and red wax used by one of their agents. "Take the elevator to the fourth floor. Chief's office is straight ahead, the last one on the left," he said dismissively then watched as Lancelot did his best not to trip as he headed for the elevator.

"The fourth floor," Lancelot repeated, leaving the comforting shadow of the front door, which immediately swung shut. He looked over his shoulder, but there wasn't a doorknob on this side either. Not that it mattered since the door locked as soon as it closed.

The elevator door, located directly ahead, automatically opened as Lancelot drew near. After his body cleared the door, it rapidly slid shut trapping him inside the confines of the elevator and blocking the image of the man staring at him. He pressed the number four then felt the smooth, remarkably fast glide upward. When the elevator reached the fourth floor, the door automatically opened. Lancelot bolted out, remembering how quickly the door shut on the ground floor.

He searched desperately for a sign that said 'Stairway,' or 'Exit' because that's where he was headed. But they obviously didn't believe in fire laws in this place because neither sign was evident.

"Chief's office is straight ahead, the last one on the left," came the voice of the man he'd just left. Once again, Lancelot looked for speakers set into the walls or ceiling. Where did his voice come from? Taking a deep, shaky breath, he soldiered on until he reached the last door on the left. It also opened in sync with his arrival.

"Step forward!" a voice said sharply.

He could stand in the hallway all day or go inside, deliver the paper, and leave—he hoped. As soon as he stepped into the room, the door closed, and that familiar click echoed in his ears.

"Who are you?" said the voice.

Lancelot faced the voice buried behind material stacked on a gigantic desk. He opened his mouth, but nothing came out. Wetting his lips, he tried again. "Lancelot Maddox."

"Step forward," the voice commanded.

Lancelot turned and looked at the door. No handle. Locked anyway.

With a kindlier tone, he repeated the command. "Step forward, please."

Lancelot stepped to the front of the desk and attempted to straighten his shoulders. There was a clear path between the middle of the desk and the man who sat on a chair. His eyes raced across its depth, coming to rest on the voice's face. The man's unblinking, steel-gray eyes bore into his.

Slowly, the man took off his half-moon glasses and leaned forward. "You're a bit young to be delivering a message, aren't you?"

"Actually, I'm fourteen."

"Didn't open it, did you?"

"No."

"Good." The man sighed then eased back into his chair. "Don't know that I've ever heard anyone called Lancelot."

Lancelot sighed. "Nobody else has either. My parents met in college. They were both actors in King Arthur and His Knights of the Round Table. Dad was King Arthur and Mom was Queen Guinevere. So, they named us Gawain, Tristam, and Lancelot after some of the knights in the play."

The man nodded sympathetically.

"It could be worse," Lancelot added. "If I'd been a girl, you'd be calling me Guinevere right now."

The bushy eyebrows fell. "Narrow escape."

"I know," Lancelot agreed. "People should be more careful what they name their children."

"Yes, I see your point." The man cleared his throat. "Well, you have something for me?"

Lancelot shoved the sealed paper across the desk.

Chief slipped on a pair of plastic evidence gloves, broke the seal, and studied it as his lips compressed. Then he peered at Lancelot. "Who gave this to you?"

Lancelot's answer may determine whether or not he left this room and building, so he kept it brief. "A woman."

"What woman?"

"Uh, she didn't tell me her name."

The man placed his forearms on the desk and leaned forward. "Think! What did she look like?"

"It's d-difficult to say," Lancelot stammered, his eyes drifting to the ceiling. "Her hair was a medium brown color. She was about three inches shorter than I am. Not too heavy or thin," he continued in a soft remembering sort of way. "She was just sort of average. Oh, and she carried a beat-up straw purse with a missing handle."

"That's very odd," the man said as his brows drew together. "No one told me Kat was back in the country. Probably receive a memo about it sometime later today. She's being followed otherwise she wouldn't have passed this onto you."

Lancelot blinked. "You know her?"

"I know her," the man said, then spread the sheet of paper flat against the desk. "But there's a problem."

"There is?"

"The message is in code. It's a very simple code because she didn't have a code book with her. Must have made this up on the run when she discovered she was being followed. She didn't want to lead them here which is why she passed it on to you. The daytime decoders left and the next shift won't report until six o'clock. I'm rather dreadful when it comes to codes," Chief said with regret.

"What kind of code is it?" Lancelot asked. "I'm good at that sort of thing."

Chief drew his brows together and studied the young man doubtfully.

"I'd like to try," Lancelot said then added. "I don't know your name."

"I'm the boss around here, so just call me Chief."

"Would you at least give me a chance, Chief?"

Chief studied the boy then signaled for Lancelot to walk around the desk. When Lancelot reached his side, Chief turned the coded message in Lancelot's direction then gave him evidence gloves to slip on.

"I already touched it."

"Yes, but you didn't touch the inside of the paper."

Lancelot slipped the evidence gloves over his hands then picked up the paper and studied the code for two full minutes. He considered each letter, it's arrangement within the group of letters, and whether it was repeated inside each section. Then, wetting his lips, he unhooked the mechanical pencil from his shirt pocket.

This was the code.

FT CBOWD JKMMKZBN WBBN CODDU TBBS TB FS CFJ-BLKPCB WOWB SKWODLS

One minute ticked by then another. By the time the third minute had completed its cycle, Lancelot returned the pencil to his shirt pocket and swiveled the paper around for Chief to read.

"AM BEING FOLLOWED NEED BIGGS MEET ME AT SAFE-HOUSE NINE TONIGHT"

Chapter 3

"I knew she was being followed or she would have come here herself rather than pass the message off to you," Chief looked up with a quizzical look on his face "Did she say who was following her?"

Lancelot shrugged. "She didn't say who was following her, but I didn't see anyone."

"They'd be a very poor excuse for a foreign agent if you could easily spot them," Chief said. "You do see that, don't you?

Lancelot thought a moment then nodded. "Yes, I can see that now."

Chief looked at the paper then back at Lancelot. "Coded messages come in about three times a week in between shifts. It can be a real problem if it's an emergency. Would you be interested in coming in and working on them?"

"You mean this time in the afternoon?"

"Yes, roughly three-thirty to six a few times a week."

Lancelot's mouth creased down, but there was a glint in his eyes.

"Well, I have soccer practice then, but they don't really need me. I'd rather solve puzzles and codes. When do you want me to start?"

"Let's begin your employment with the agency the last week of August?"

"When school starts?"

"If that's convenient."

"Oh, yes!" Lancelot said, a little louder than he'd intended. "I just wondered…"

"About what?"

"I suppose this is, uh, top secret?"

"Absolutely top secret only spouses know. Well, and parents in your case. We insist on all employees signing a Pledge of Confidentiality."

"I'll only tell my parents and no one else," Lancelot promised.

"Very well," Chief said. He opened a drawer at the side of his desk and withdrew a long sheet of paper written in fine print with a line at the bottom for a signature. "This is the Pledge of Confidentiality form all new employees sign. Signing this indicates you will at no time reveal any information you see, hear, or discover while employed at this intelligence agency or after you leave this agency." Chief leaned forward. "Do you understand the seriousness of what I just said Lancelot? If so, signify by saying 'I do'."

Lancelot swallowed hard wondering if those were the best or worst two words he would ever utter. Drawing himself up to his full height, he said, "I do."

Chief flipped the paper towards Lancelot and handed him a pen. After the form was signed, he pressed a button and a small rectangular-shaped box buried inside Chief's desk rose above the surface. It had three small drawers. He opened the top one, withdrew a small stiff card, then pressed the same button and the box lowered again. Picking up his green-ink pen, he wrote 'Lancelot Maddox' on the top line, then signed it at the bottom with the letter 'C'. "This is your identity card," he said, pressing it toward Lancelot. "Mr. Biggs is head of security. You met him at the door when you arrived. You'll need to present this ID card to him to verify who you are."

"Yes, Chief," Lancelot said. He blew on the ink until it was dry. Then, with great care, he placed it in a billfold he kept in his side pocket.

"You will report for your first day of work as a part-time decoder on Monday the last week of August at three-thirty sharp."

"Yes, Chief. Do I report to this room?"

"No. Mr. Biggs will let you into the building, check your ID card, and take you to the decoding room on the ground floor."

"Yes, Chief," Lancelot said.

Chief was about to return to his work when he picked up the decoded message. "Lancelot, give the message you decoded to Mr. Biggs on your way out. He needs to know about this immediately. I'll send someon to pick it up so we can check it for fingerprints."

Lancelot slipped on his evidence gloves again, grasped the brown paper, and carried it out the door. At the ground floor, he strode purposefully to Mr. Biggs' office where the head of security looked up. "Chief said to give this to you, uh, Mr. Biggs."

Mr. Biggs looked at the boy for a second then slipped on evidence gloves from a side drawer. "Nine tonight," he murmured. "Did you decode this message?”

“Just now in Chief’s office.” Suddenly, Lancelot remembered his ID card. He withdrew it from his billfold and handed it to the head of security.

Mr. Biggs glanced at it then looked up. “Hired you on the spot?”

“Chief hired me on the spot,” Lancelot said, with an unfamiliar note of pride in his voice.

Mr. Biggs studied the boy then said, “Welcome aboard, kid.”

Thanks,” Lancelot said then stepped back expecting Mr. Biggs to usher him into the hallway where the head of security would punch in the code to open the door. But he didn’t. He examined the decoded message then lifted his eyes to stare at Lancelot. It was quite unsettling to be stared at with that level of scrutiny.

“Where did you get this?”

“At the park.”

“How long ago,” Mr. Biggs said.

Lancelot glanced at his watch. “About an hour ago.”

“What did the person look like who gave you this message?

“Well, I already described her to Chief,” Lancelot said.

“Describe her to me,” Mr. Biggs said nicely, but there was an air of authority about him.

“Well, she was about three inches shorter than I am, brownish hair. Not too thin or heavy, just sort of average.” He hesitated then remembered what feature had enlightened Chief. “She carried an old straw purse with a missing handle.”

Mr. Biggs slowly nodded. “Missing handle,” he murmured. “Look, kid. Where in the park did you meet her?"

"I was almost in the center of the park sitting on a bench working on my puzzles when she came up to me."

"Okay. Just tell me everything you can remember."

Lancelot drew his brows together. "She walked up to me and pretended to know me. I'd never met her before in my life. She sat down and wanted me to laugh with her. Said someone dangerous was following her. I couldn't see anyone, but she didn't want me to look around."

When Lancelot hesitated, Mr. Biggs said, "You're doing great, kid. What else happened?"

"She wanted me to walk around the pond with her then she told me to take her hand. That's when she passed the note to me. She gave me the address to this building and told me to take the note there. She said not to worry, because they would follow her and not me. So, that's what I did. I brought the note here then decoded it for Chief."

"Good. Now, this is important, kid. Take your time and tell me if you think this woman was really frightened or was she pretending to be frightened? Was it just an act or was she afraid?"

Lancelot hadn't thought about it until the head of security brought it up. Was it an act or was she really frightened? He didn't feel comfortable around people, yet he could read people fairly well. "I think," he began slowly. "she was just pretending to be frightened."

"Why do you say that?" Mr. Biggs said.

"Her hands weren't shaking and she wasn't sweating. When she handed me the message, her hands were dry. Her voice didn't tremble like someone who is really scared."

Mr. Biggs nodded with that look of triumph. "I knew it," he said softly. He sat down and drummed his fingertips on his desk. Suddenly, he typed in a series of letters and numbers and a new screen popped up. He clicked through various screens until he found what he was looking for. "Okay, kid. Come around here and tell me if this is the woman you saw."

Chapter 4

Lancelot studied the screen trying to decide if there was any similarity between the woman on the screen and the woman he spoke to at the park. Finally, he turned to Mr. Biggs and said, "No, that's not the woman I saw."

"Someone posing as Kat," Mr. Biggs whispered. "I didn't know she was back in the country."

"That's what Chief said. He didn't know she was back in the country either."

Someone came through the elevator door and a woman appeared at the doorway. "Chief said he wanted something fingerprinted."

"Right, thanks," Mr. Biggs said, handing her the coded message. After she left, he pushed away from his desk. "I want you to take me to the place where she approached you."

"Okay, I'll take you there."

Mr. Biggs open a cabinet drawer and slipped something into his pocket then punched in a code which opened the front door. Within minutes, they stood in front of the bench where Lancelot had sat so peacefully only a short time earlier. The head of security surveyed the area with practiced eyes. "Did she sit down beside you?"

"Yes," Lancelot said with a certain amount of distaste.

"What did she touch?"

"Touch?"

"Right. When she sat down, did she touch anything?"

Lancelot replayed the scene in his mind. "Nothing. She didn't touch anything." He thought a few seconds then added, "Fingerprints! Right? You're thinking about fingerprints."

The tiniest of smiles formed on Mr. Biggs' lips. "That's good, kid. I'm looking for fingerprints."

"What about my fingerprints on the message I delivered?"

"You only touched the part with red wax. They'll check for fingerprints on the paper itself," Mr. Biggs said. "You said you walked around, right?"

"Yes, we walked around that pond but she didn't touch anything there either."

Mr. Biggs continued to search the surrounding area.

Lancelot used that period of time to study the head of security and think through what was happening. This was a puzzle. He'd solved puzzles for years. But those were in his puzzle books. It took several minutes, but he finally figured it out. "You think she's an imposter. You think the woman who gave me the message isn't who Chief thinks she is."

Mr. Biggs slowly turned around and gave Lancelot a hard look. "You know something, kid? You're young, but you're very sharp." He hesitated as he continued to stare at Lancelot. "Meet me here at eight fifteen tonight. Okay?"

"Okay," Lancelot said softly. "I'll be here at eight fifteen tonight."

"Good. Wear dark clothes." Mr. Biggs waited until Lancelot nodded then turned on his heel and headed back to the intelligence agency.

Lancelot's eyes followed him until he was out of sight. Dark clothes. Was this some type of intelligence mission or whatever they called it? He'd find out tonight.

Lancelot retraced his steps to home. As he strolled mindlessly along, a thought occurred to him. Why did the woman at the park want the head of security to meet her rather than an agent? He knew nothing about how an intelligence agency was run, but it did seem odd that the head of security would work with agents. He shrugged hoping he'd find out later. He was to be at the park at eight fifteen. The coded message said to meet at the safehouse at nine. What was going to happen in those forty-five minutes?

Lancelot walked through the front door and drifted back the hallway to his mother's office, but it was empty. The entire house was empty, so he made his way up the stairs to his room and tried to remember how he solved the puzzle he was so anxious to write down when that woman so rudely interrupted him. Had she interrupted him or changed the course of his life? It didn't seem to matter now. He sat at his desk and stared out the window wondering how his parents would feel about him working at an intelligence agency. He'd find out after dinner that night. Meanwhile, he changed into a dark shirt and sweatpants.

Strangely enough, or perhaps not so strangely, his parents accepted the idea. They even seemed relieved that Lancelot reacted with so much enthusiasm concerning the job offer. So, they didn't say a word when he left shortly after eight o'clock. It was still daylight, but the early evening shadows had made their way into the park. As he walked along, he continued to wonder why Mr. Biggs needed him? What could a fourteen-year-old boy add to the situation. When he arrived at the exact spot where he met the woman, Mr. Biggs was waiting for him in equally dark clothes.

It finally occurred to Lancelot why Mr. Biggs needed him. "You want me to identify whether the woman at the safehouse is the same woman I saw here at the park, right?"

The crease in his mouth that passed for a smile formed on Mr. Biggs' lips again. "That's the reason, kid."

Lancelot straightened his shoulders. "What do you want me to do?"

The smile disappeared. Mr. Biggs' mind focused on what was ahead. "I'll fill you in as we go."

Lancelot fell into step with the head of security. They walked softly but with purpose out of the park and down the dimly lit street. As they rounded a corner into an even darker street, Mr. Biggs said, "Most of our agents are ordinary-looking people who blend in with the crowd and are difficult to describe because there is nothing unusual about them. The agent who carries a purse with only one handle is exactly like that. Only an insider at the intelligence agency knows who she is."

"I get it. Describing her is like describing a million other women."

"Right. That's why she carries a purse with one handle. Most women would buy another purse or have the missing handle replaced."

"I still don't get it. What made you suspect she's an imposter?"

Mr. Biggs glanced at Lancelot, then said, "I was her contact for five years. When they transferred her abroad to work, she was assigned to someone else, so that's the person she should have contacted. But the imposter didn't know that. It's either that or someone specifically wants me there tonight. That's why I needed you to look at her photo on my computer screen."

"Are you worried?" Lancelot asked softly.

"In this business, we're always worried, kid. If you stop worrying, you let your guard down, and that's when you miss something. When you miss something, it usually means somebody gets hurt."

A thought occurred to Lancelot, but he was hesitant to ask.

Sensing his anxiety, Mr. Biggs said, "What is it, kid?"

"Well, uh, I just wonder how you thought she might be an imposter, but Chief didn't."

"Good question. When Kat was assigned abroad, Chief didn't reassign her to someone else. A supervisor at Headquarters did that. So, that's the person she should have asked for in the coded message rather than me. Chief undoubtedly thought she was reassigned back here and figured I was her contact again. He probably thinks he'll get a memo on it sometime today," Mr. Biggs said.

"That's what he told me," Lancelot said.

"In this business, you're always looking for something out of the ordinary or unusual or doesn't follow the normal sequence of events.

Understand?"

Lancelot studied Mr. Biggs for a moment. "I understand," he said softly.

They moved silently along the narrow, dimly lit street always keeping within the shadows until they came to a car parked in the driveway of an abandoned house. "Wait here," Mr. Biggs said softly.

Lancelot squinted into the darkness and made out four figures inside the car. There may have been more, but that's all he saw. They all leaned forward listening to what the head of security had to say as if he were the most important person in the world. Who were they? Mr. Biggs hadn't said anything about other people meeting them here. But he'd been employed by the agency for only a few hours, so he wasn't really entitled to know secret information pertaining to a mission. He was lucky he'd been asked to join. But would he still feel lucky two hours from now?

Lancelot watched as Mr. Biggs leaned his hands on the roof of the car while the people whispered back and forth. Then something rather odd happened. As he was ready to leave, the men in the car saluted him and Mr. Biggs returned their salute. Were they retired military people? Who else would salute like that?

When Mr. Biggs returned, Lancelot said, "Do they work at the agency?"

"No."

"Oh, well, who are…"

"Don't ask, kid."

As they crept farther down the street, Lancelot faintly heard car doors opening and closing. He waited for the sound of footsteps, but they didn't come. It was unnerving being around professionals at this level. Everybody made some noise when they moved, but not these people. At the moment, his were the only footsteps loud enough to be heard. He softened each footstep as it touched the ground. He was learning.

A block later, Mr. Biggs slipped behind a line of bushes. He dropped down then parted the bushes an inch and stared without blinking at a darkened house across the street and two houses down from where they were. Was it the safehouse? Did he dare ask?

Lancelot saw movement out of the corner of his eye. But when he turned his head, no one was there. Had it been one of the people from the car? Or one of the people connected to the imposter? His eyes returned to the house waiting for something to happen.

Mr. Biggs reached for the phone vibrating inside his pocket. He listened then replaced it without saying anything. "Let's go," he whispered.

Chapter 5

Lancelot trailed after him as they headed away from the safety of cover.

When they reached the end of the street, Mr. Biggs suddenly turned to him. "You signed the Pledge of Confidentiality form, right?" When Lancelot nodded, Mr. Biggs said. "Do you understand that you are never to reveal anything you've seen, heard, or discovered while employed by the intelligence agency or after you leave the employment of this agency."

"Yes, I understand that."

"Do you understand what it means?"

"I am never to tell anyone anything about what happens either while I'm working for the agency or after I leave."

Mr. Biggs gave the young decoder a piercing look then crossed the street and turned left into an alley that bordered the back of the house they'd kept under surveillance for the past fifteen minutes. Were they going in through the back door?

Mr. Biggs kept to the edge of the alley where the grass silenced their movement. There were no streetlights down the alley. The only light came from kitchens located at the back of the houses. Even then, there were a few garages dotted along the alley. When they came to a garage, it cut off any the light to the house beyond it.

Mr. Biggs stopped behind the only completely darkened house on either side of the alley.

"Is that the house," Lancelot whispered.

Mr. Biggs nodded, then crossed the alley and stood in front of a garage directly across from where the safehouse stood. Surely this garage belonged to the people behind the garage, not to the safehouse across the alley. But Mr. Biggs withdrew a key from his pocket and silently unlocked the door, and just as silently opened it.

Inside, it was pitch black. Lancelot lightly ran his fingers around the wall looking for a light switch, but Mr. Biggs whispered, "It needs to be dark in here."

"What do we do now?"

"We wait."

Lancelot hesitated but it never hurts to ask. "What are we waiting for?"

"We're waiting to see if she uses the front door to get in."

"Isn't that what everyone does?" Lancelot said. "Are you saying she shouldn't use the front door to get into the house?"

"Right, she shouldn't use the front door," Mr. Biggs said. "Look, kid.

You've got a right to know what's going on. The reason we're waiting to see if anybody uses the front door is because nobody uses the front door except a few times each week during the daytime just so the neighbors think somebody actually lives here and don't become suspicious."

"Okay, I get that part. If nobody lived there, they'd wonder what was going on."

"All the agents come and go from the safehouse at night. They gain entrance through a tunnel that begins inside this garage, runs underneath the alley and into the basement of the safehouse. There are only a few people who know about it and Kat is one of them."

"The agency dug a tunnel all the way from here to the basement of that house?"

"No. It was already here. That's why we bought the house," Mr. Biggs said.

"Already here? Why would someone dig a tunnel from the garage to the house?"

Mr. Biggs hesitated then said. "It was part of the Underground Railroad system way back in the eighteen hundreds. Only a handful of people knew about it then and only a few people at the agency are aware it even exists. We found out about it and knew it was perfect for a safehouse."

Lancelot marveled at what he had just learned but only for a moment.

"That's why we're waiting in the dark. I'm hoping the woman you saw will come through the garage door because she knows about the tunnel."

Lancelot stood motionless as his eyes adjusted to the darkness.

There was just enough light in the garage to see the outline of objects hanging on nails around the wall and scattered on the floor. He could just make out the expression on Mr. Biggs' face. His face was tight but under control.

"Your friends are at the front watching for her. If she walks in the front door, then you know she's not part of the intelligence agency. If she walks in here, then everything is okay."

"That's what we're hoping, kid That she'll walk through this door," Mr. Biggs said softly. "The only exception would be if she's already in the house."

"The key. If agents always enter the house through the tunnel in this garage, how is she going to get in the front door without a key?"

"They have a key. There's also a code they can punch in if they don't have their key. Occasionally, they'll bring someone here who doesn't know about the tunnel, but they only keep that person in the safehouse for a short time."

"I get it," Lancelot said.

The phone vibrated. "Biggs," he whispered. In the dimness of the garage, Lancelot saw him lower his head and tighten his lips. "Right. Thanks, Bake."

Lancelot waited. When no information was forthcoming, he said, "What happened?"

"Bake saw the curtain move on the second floor."

"Bake?"

Mr. Biggs hesitated then said, "His name's Baker. He's an old army buddy of mine."

Then Mr. Baker's message struck him. "Someone's inside the house," Lancelot whispered. "Waiting for us."

"No," Mr. Biggs said. "They're waiting for me."

Lancelot was speechless. "This whole thing was set up as a trap to catch you?"

"Right," Mr. Biggs said as if he expected it.

"I wonder how many there are?"

"Won't know until I go inside."

Lancelot appreciated the darkness when he felt his face pale. "We're going inside?"

Mr. Biggs glanced at the young decoder. "Just me for now. Bake and the boys will hold off for ten minutes until I see what's happening," he said. "You'll wait here until everything settles then you'll come in the house and identify the woman you saw at the park. If she's there."

Lancelot couldn't decide whether to be relieved or disappointed. His emotions finally settled somewhere in between. "If I went along, maybe I could help."

Mr. Biggs shook his head. "You're not trained. You wouldn't know what to do."

"But why is Mr. Baker holding off for ten minutes?" Lancelot said, trying and failing to keep his voice steady. "Shouldn't they go in with you in case there's trouble?"

"They're expecting me to come in alone. When I show up by myself, they'll relax just enough that when Bake and the boys show up, we can catch them off guard."

"Do you think it will work?"

"No idea, kid."

He drew out his phone and punched in a number. "Bake?" he whispered. "I'm going in. I'll be through the tunnel and into the basement in sixty seconds."

Lancelot's eyes widened. "You're leaving now?"

"Leaving now. You stay here," Mr. Biggs said, then handed Lancelot his phone. "If you haven't heard from me or Bake in fifteen minutes, call Chief. Just press number one and he'll answer."

Lancelot's trembling hands grasped the phone then looked up. "Will Chief know what to do?"

"He'll know what to do."

"But does Chief know you're here?"

"He knows," Mr. Biggs said. "No more questions." He grabbed two flashlights off a ledge, handed one to Lancelot, then lifted a door in the floor and climbed down the ladder far enough that his head cleared the level of the floor. Slowly and soundlessly, he lowered the door to cover the opening into the tunnel.

Chapter 6

Even though the darkness had been their friend, Lancelot suddenly felt vulnerable and afraid. What if the secret of the garage had leaked out and the wrong people showed up here? His eyes tracked slowly around the room looking for the dim outline of an object that resembled a weapon. Finally, he settled on a broom used to clear the garage doorway of leaves and debris. It was absolutely pathetic as weapons go, but it was better than what he had now which was nothing.

Lancelot pushed open the door far enough to see the safehouse. His lips formed a straight line as he thought of what Mr. Biggs might face and how he was going to handle it. The head of security had been right. He'd have no idea what to do in a tight situation like this.

Suddenly, a small crease of light seeped in between the curtains in the back of the house. It was probably the kitchen. Enough time had passed that Mr. Biggs was there, but what was happening? Lancelot saw the curtains rustle violently as if people were fighting and kept bumping into it. But who were the people and which person was winning?

Mr. Baker and his men weren't due in the house for at least seven or eight minutes. They were at the front of the house and had no idea there was a struggle in the kitchen. And Mr. Biggs was alone.

With total disregard for orders, Lancelot dropped to his knees brushing his hand along the floor but couldn't find the ring to pull up the door leading into the tunnel. He shielded the flashlight, so the beam fell squarely on the floor. As soon as he found the ring, he shut off the flashlight, and pulled the door open. Pressing the broom against the side of his body, his foot tapped the air until he found the first rung. Then step by tedious step, he made his way down the ladder until his head cleared the floor, then lowered the door again.

It wasn't easy climbing down the ladder with the broom clasped between his arm and his body while holding the flashlight with the same hand. The other hand hung onto each rung while his foot stepped precariously down until he reached the floor of the tunnel. The tunnel was musty as only an old, closed-in place can smell. Lancelot turned on the flashlight and moved forward until he came to a door. What was on the other side? Did it lead into the basement as Mr. Biggs had suggested? He was below the surface of the ground, so it had to be the basement. Would the hinges squeak? He'd find out shortly.

He turned off the flashlight and slowly pushed open the door. It was soundless. Without realizing it, he'd been holding his breath. He stepped through and closed the door but all he heard were loud footsteps pounding the floor above.

Lancelot swung the flashlight around the room until he found the stairs then raced across the dirt floor taking the steps two at a time. He slowly opened the door and peeked through the crack. It was Mr. Biggs and an unknown person engaged in an even match.

For a moment, Lancelot stood in amazement. The other man was much younger than Mr. Biggs, but the head of security was holding his own in this battle, at least for now.

Lancelot was not a violent person. He avoided any kind of altercation. He considered his options, then waited until the younger man's back was to him. Taking two steps into the room, he used the broom handle to tap the man rather vigorously on the shoulder.

The young man turned around with a shocked look on his face. It was at that moment Mr. Biggs used a perfected side kick resulting in the man's immediate shift from standing to lying flat on the floor in a half stupor. Exhausted, the younger man lay on his side dazed with his eyes closed.

Mr. Biggs rolled him over onto his stomach then placed his foot on his back so the man couldn't get up. "Give me the phone," he said. After Lancelot handed it to him, he punched in a number. "Bake? Two of you come to the backdoor. I've got a guy you need to take away."

Hardly a minute passed when the backdoor opened and two men about Mr. Biggs' age stepped through. "There are others upstairs, Bake. Tell the guys to wait outside the front door." The one who must have been Mr. Baker nodded his head. Then, without uttering a word, they took the man outside leaving as silently as they came.

Mr. Biggs sat heavily on a chair at the table with Lancelot sitting across from him. "Why didn't someone from upstairs come down to help when they heard the fighting."

"Didn't hear us. When the house was purchased, they soundproofed some of the rooms and the kitchen was one of them."

Soundproofed? This agency business was going to take some getting used to. "Do you know how many people are upstairs?"

Mr. Biggs' breath was coming under control now. "No idea, but I'd guess no more than three or four others, I hope," he said. "They weren't sure which door I'd use, so he rotated between the front door and the kitchen. He was shocked when I walked through the basement door. That gave me just enough time to knock the gun out of his hand. That's when the fighting started."

"Since you came up through the basement, I wonder if they'll find out about the tunnel," Lancelot said.

"I doubt it. He thinks I was down there hiding." With his breathing restored to normal, Mr. Biggs and Lancelot's eyes met across the table. Would the head of security scold or congratulate him? "Good work, kid," he said softly.

A smile began to lighten Lancelot's face, then he remembered the others upstairs. "Don't you think we need help from Mr. Baker right now?"

"Got a plan. Need another minute to think it through." Mr. Biggs rubbed his chin as he studied the newly hired decoder. He considered his build, hair color, and approximate height and weight.

"What?" Lancelot said. "What are you thinking?"

"I'm thinking," Mr. Biggs began. "I'm thinking you and that man I fought with are about the same size. Your hair is about the same color, too."

Lancelot wasn't quite sure where this was headed, but his stomach was definitely concerned about it. "Uh, is that important?"

Mr. Biggs' eyes bore into Lancelot's testing whether or not this young kid was up to the strategy he had just created. "Did you notice if the upstairs lights are on?"

Lancelot's mind drifted back to what he observed peeking through the garage door. "No. Only the kitchen lights were on in the back."

"They didn't turn on any lights in the back rooms, and they'd never turn on lights in rooms facing the front. So, the only light coming into the rooms upstairs are from the streetlights. It'll be just dim enough that you might get away with it."

Lancelot was a sharp young man, and it took him exactly three seconds to figure this out. "You want me to impersonate that guy you were fighting, right?"

"For a few minutes," Mr. Biggs said. "I don't know how many people are up there. What we need to do is reduce the numbers."

"How are we going to reduce the numbers? Am I going to have to tackle somebody?"

Mr. Biggs swallowed a chuckle as he shook his head. "You're the thinking type, kid. What you are going to do is create enough suspicion in their minds that one of them will come down to check on whether or not you're telling the truth." He studied the broom laying on the floor then picked it up. "This might work."

"The broom might work. How?"

"You'll see," Mr. Biggs said.

"You can't whack anyone very hard with a broom like that."

"I don't intend to whack anyone, kid," Mr. Biggs said then returned to his plan. "Now, once someone comes down the stairs, the boys outside will grab him, then that's one person we won't have to worry about."

"And my job is to create enough curiosity about something that somebody will want to come down and check it out."

"That will be your job," Mr. Biggs said.

Chapter 7

Lancelot stalled by nodding his head. "But my clothes are different. Even in the dim light, don't you think they'll notice that?"

"Look behind you. His hat and jacket are on the floor. Try them on. See how they fit."

Lancelot picked up the two items the man had tossed in a corner. As he tried them on, he pondered the following. If this was how his first five hours on the job were like, what did his future hold with the intelligence agency? It didn't escape him that he'd have to survive the next few hours in order to have a future of any kind.

After Lancelot slid his arms through the jacket and donned the hat, the head of security closed his eyes halfway and studied the effect. "Stand up a little straighter and pull your hat farther down on your head." Having done that, Mr. Biggs nodded. "It'll work for a few seconds and that's all we need."

"Okay," Lancelot said, making a valiant effort not to crumble. "What do you want me to do?"

After Mr. Biggs laid out the strategy and the layout of the upstairs was explained, Lancelot said, "The kitchen is soundproof, so they won't know I'm lying, right?"

"Right, they'll have to come downstairs to find out," Mr. Biggs said. He picked up his phone, pressed a number then said, "Are you stationed at the front door, Bake? Good."

Slowly, Lancelot rose to his feet and walked to the bottom of the stairs, then waited until Mr. Biggs unlocked the front door and opened it an inch. Mr. Biggs gave the boy an encouraging pat on the back while Lancelot mentally rehearsed what he had to do.

Taking a deep breath, Lancelot bounded up the stairs screaming at the top of his lungs, "I shot him! I think he's dead! There's blood all over the place!" He kept repeating this as he raced to the end of the hallway and into the bathroom, and locked it.

Footsteps rushed down the hallway and pounded on the bathroom door. At the sound of footsteps, Mr. Biggs stepped back and waited. Within seconds, someone came stumbling down the stairs. As soon as he reached the third step from the bottom, Mr. Biggs shoved the broom handle between the stairway rails and caught the man's foot midstride. The man tried to catch himself but fell hard knocking the wind out of him.

Mr. Baker and another man quietly picked him up and ushered him through the door, while he was still too dazed to react. "Two down," Mr. Baker said.

People still pounded on the bathroom door trying to convince the person inside to open the door.

Mr. Biggs tightened his grip on the broom then took the stairs two at a time. He peered down the hallway to see how many people there were. Two men tried to out scream Lancelot who put everything he had into his assigned role. He peeked around a corner and looked through a bedroom door where a dim light shone from a single lamp.

A woman sitting on a chair caught movement in the doorway and looked up then quickly looked down again. She pressed her lips into a straight line as she thought. Her head turned sideways then faced the doorway again. Her eyes flicked to the side. Someone else was in the room with her.

Mr. Biggs slipped into the bedroom next door. From the darkness of that room, he had a good view of the room where Kat was held prisoner. He saw the profile of the other woman then she glanced at the men pounding on the bathroom door. She was the imposter. Lancelot's description fit the woman perfectly.

As soon as the imposter turned away, Mr. Biggs quickly devised a plan to further decrease the numbers. He caught Kat's eye then mimicked putting something into his mouth. He grabbed his throat and coughed silently then flung his hand to the side knocking over an invisible glass of water. Next, he used his index and middle fingers to give the impression of someone walking down the stairs.

Kat glanced at the imposter who was standing at the window peeking through the blinds. She reached for a cracker resting at her elbow, bit off a corner then began to cough. In reaching for a glass of water, she knocked it over. Her coughing grew louder but wasn't heard outside the room because of the tremendous noise created at the end of the hallway.

The imposter stepped forward then waited to see if Kat would recover. In between gasps, Kat said, "Water! I need water!"

Mr. Biggs sent a text message that read. "Imposter may head down steps."

With a disgusted swipe of her hand, the imposter picked up the glass and headed down the hall to the bathroom. "She's chocking! I need water!" she said, roaring above the racket.

"You'll have to go downstairs to get it!" one of the men yelled.

Stomping back to the bedroom, the imposter stood in the doorway and pointed a finger at Kat. "Don't move!" When she reached the last step, the front door open and she disappeared.

A thin smile formed on Mr. Biggs' lips as he saw Bake and the boys take another person into custody. Three down, two to go.

The two men turned sideways and used their combined strength to break down the door as Lancelot's voice grew increasingly hoarse from the screaming.

Mr. Biggs slipped into the other bedroom and walked directly to where Kat sat. "Are you all right?"

"Yes," Kat said. "They called yesterday and told me to take the next flight here. Said you had information for my ears alone. I got here during the day, so I used the front door." She shook her head. "It was a trap."

"For both of us," Mr. Biggs said. "I wonder why they singled us out."

Before Kat could respond, the two men in the hallway broke through the bathroom door. There was silence until they recovered from the shock of seeing someone they didn't expect.

Lancelot stepped back until he hit the wall and could move no farther then stared at the two men as he willed his legs not to fold.

"Sit tight," Mr. Biggs whispered then crouched beside the door with his broom handle at the ready.

Kat sat back in her chair and continued to cough.

For a moment, the men stared at a perfect stranger. "Who are you?" one man demanded.

"Me? W-well," Lancelot began as his mind froze. "I'm not really s-sure. I just got hired and…"

"You're wearing Stan's jacket," the man said. "Where is he? What have you done with him?"

"Done with him?" Lancelot said, pushing up his glasses. "I haven't done anything with him. Somebody just took him away. That's about all I can tell you." At that terrifying moment, he wondered whether everyone had forgotten about him and left.

The man shoved Lancelot through the bathroom door then grabbed his arm as he marched down the hallway with the other man trailing behind. Kat sat coughing while she watched them approach.

Even in his frantic state of mind, Lancelot realized he'd seen the woman sitting in the chair before. Then it came to him. She was the woman on Mr. Biggs' computer screen. The head of security had pulled up her image wondering if she was the woman who handed him the coded message in the park. But the woman in the park was very ordinary looking. This woman was more attractive.

But where was Mr. Biggs? Had they both been left to fend for themselves? He had only known the head of security a few hours but he refused to believe Mr. Biggs would desert anyone.

As soon as Lancelot and the man gripping his arm cleared the door, Mr. Biggs waited for the second man's foot to cross the threshold then shoved the broom between his feet. Like the man on the staircase, he fell flat on his face.

When the first man turned around, he loosened his grip on Lancelot's arm and the young decoder jerked his arm free and quickly stepped to Kat's side.. "Biggs!" he said through slitted eyes.

"That's right," Mr. Biggs said softly.

Before the man on the floor could recover, Mr. Baker and one of his men appeared through the door, yanked the man to his feet and ushered him down the steps and through the front door.

"You wanted to know who this young man is," Mr. Biggs said, nodding at Lancelot. "He's with me."

The other man searched the room and discovered his entire team had vanished. "What have you done with the others?"

"They're gone. You're the only one left," Mr. Biggs said.

"Where are they?"

Mr. Biggs shook his head. "No idea. They'll be out of the way for a long time, so it doesn't matter where they are right now. What's the purpose of all this?"

The man pressed his lips into a thin line. "You'll find out. You won't find out now, but you'll find out someday. We won't let this happen again," he said, casting a glance at Kat then back at Mr. Biggs.

Two of Mr. Baker's men came into the room, but the man refused to allow them to take his arms. He walked out of the room and down the steps with his head held high.

Kat rose and allowed Lancelot to collapse onto the chair. "Are you all right?" she said, placing her hand on his shoulder.

"I don't know," Lancelot said. "I think so."

"What's your name?"

"Lancelot Maddox. Chief hired me a few hours ago. I'm all confused. I thought I was supposed to decode messages."

Kat looked at Mr. Biggs and the barest of smiles crossed their lips. "Well, you were splendid, Lancelot. You are a very brave young man and we're all very proud of you."

Suddenly, the past few hours disappeared under Kat's warm voice. "Really?"

"Yes, really." Kat glanced at Mr. Biggs who gave her a head signal. "You sit tight for a few minutes, Lancelot. I need to talk to Goliath." They met in the hallway where they both glanced at Lancelot to make sure he was recovering.

"Why do you think they staged this?" Kat said.

"I don't know. It worries me because I suspect others are planning the same thing and we won't know when or where they'll strike next."

They stood a moment longer immersed in theories until Kat glanced at Lancelot's dropping shoulders. "Better take him home, Goliath. It's been a big night for him."

Mr. Biggs led him down the steps and out the front door where Mr. Baker stood with the other woman. Once Lancelot identified her as the person he saw at the park, she was led away.

Even in his foggy state of mind, Lancelot remembered this was a safehouse. "The neighbors will wonder what's going on with all these people coming and going."

"We'll create a cover story for what happened tonight." They walked in silence until they reached the park. "You were great, kid. A trained agent couldn't have done any better than you did tonight."

Lancelot's head slowly lifted. "Really? Do you mean that?"

"I do. Now, your house isn't far from here. Can you make it home on your own?"

Lancelot felt strengthened by Mr. Biggs' words. "I can make it," he said, softly. "I have a question." When Mr. Biggs lifted an eyebrow, Lancelot continued. "Why did Kat call you Goliath."

The kid had sharp ears. "It's a code name from years ago," Mr. Biggs said then vanished into the darkness.

As Lancelot listened to the echo of his footsteps in the still night air, he wondered how Mr. Biggs knew where he lived. It all happened so quickly, yet the head of security seemed to be on top of everything. Nothing rattled him. He planned everything in a few short hours. And no one got hurt. Goliath was his code name. Goliath was a giant. Was that the meaning behind his code name?

Lancelot turned and headed for home. He later discovered her name was Katherine Stephens. Kat said he was a very brave young man, and they were all very proud of him. Even though his body still trembled slightly, his lips widened into a smile.

Mr. Biggs and Kat seemed very close as if they'd been through a great deal together and formed a bond. Would he and Mr. Biggs ever see her again. Two months later, their paths would cross once more.

The Thirty-Minute Spy

At three fifteen, Lancelot dug out his ID card and pressed the buzzer at the intelligence agency. The door swung soundlessly open then soundlessly closed once he crossed the threshold. He shifted his backpack to the other shoulder as Mr. Biggs, head of security, came out of his office.

"Look, kid. You've been on the job for two weeks now. You don't need to show your ID card unless someone else is on duty."

"Okay. I don't need to dig out my ID card unless there's a substitute on duty. I get it." He strolled back the hallway stopping at the office next to his. The door, which was always open, was closed. Quietly testing the handle, he noted it was also locked. Pivoting on his heel, he returned to the front of the hallway and stood in Mr. Biggs' doorway. "Where's the duty officer?"

"Called in sick."

"Sick? Did he say what's wrong?"

"Stomach virus."

Lancelot screwed up his face. "I'm glad he stayed home."

"So am I."

Lancelot lingered in the doorway building up his courage to ask a question he wasn't sure the head of security would answer.

"What is it, kid?"

"Well," Lancelot said, shifting from one foot to the other. "I just wondered how long you work in army intelligence?"

Mr. Biggs knew the kid would find out sooner or later anyway. "Worked in army intelligence for thirty years then retired to this job at the agency."

"Army intelligence. That's a big deal."

"Can be. Often, it's just gathering information, so we know what's happening in the world rather than a bunch of fancy stuff you see in movies." When Lancelot continued to stand in the doorway, Mr. Biggs said, "Something else?"

"I just wondered if you were a part of covert operations like rescuing people or spying on people."

"Do you remember what signing the Pledge of Confidentiality means?"

"It means I can't disclose any information revealed to me or I discover while I work here or after I leave the intelligence agency."

"Right. When I worked for army intelligence, I signed something like that as well." Having said that, Mr. Biggs returned to his computer screen.

"Oh. Right. Okay," Lancelot said softly, then drifted down the hallway to the decoding room wondering what unbelievably exciting stories were locked up in Mr. Biggs' head that only a few knew about. He sat down at his desk and drew several sheets of paper off the top of the inbox. Once decoded, he normally took the messages to the duty officer of the day, who determined if it was an emergency or could wait until the following day. If it was an all-out emergency, he'd notify Chief. So far, nothing had been an emergency, so Lancelot wasn't really worried.

First two codes were short and easy, and he put them in the outbox positioned on a corner of his desk. The third message was longer.

EXWIFH OF VXYCXLX WDXHO TFSX HWBX PCEXPYM AWIICHD CHPF OF XHXBM. WDXHO PCEXPYM IOWMCHD WO BWCH IOEXXO RFOXY.

ITRRXSZYXS OF BXXO XHXBM WDXHO WO ZHCHFEH YFTWOCFH WO ILSOXXH RZHSEXS RFZEI OFSWM.

PFYYFQ! OWCX ARFOF FP RWHSFPP

Ten minutes later, Lancelot read the decoded message then read it again. He pushed up his glasses as beads of perspiration gathered on his forehead. Stumbling down the hallway, he entered the head of security's office.

Mr. Biggs studied Lancelot's flushed face and widened eyes. "What's the matter, kid?"

Lancelot swallowed. "The duty officer isn't here."

"I know. What's the problem?"

"We need to call Chief!" he said.

"Look, kid, Chief is at a meeting across town. Now what is the problem?"

Lancelot steadied his trembling hands and read the message aloud.

"REASON TO BELIEVE AGENT CODE NAME FIREFLY PASSING INFO TO ENEMY. AGENT FIREFLY STAYING AT MAIN STREET HOTEL.

SCHEDULED TO MEET ENEMY AT UNKNOWN LOCATION AT SIXTEEN HUNDRED HOURS TODAY.

FOLLOW! TAKE PHOTO OF HANDOFF."

Mr. Biggs grabbed the paper, his eyes flying over the words twice. "Sixteen hundred hours. That's four o'clock," he said absently, then consulted his watch. "Only leaves us twenty-five minutes to plan."

The blood drained from Lancelot's face. "Us? I-I don't understand what you mean by 'us'."

"Who is Firefly?" Mr. Biggs' relaxed manner disappeared. His eyes sharpened with his voice.

"If you don't know can't we just…"

"Stay with me, kid," Mr. Biggs ordered then typed in a password which brought up photos plus the code names and true identities of agents. When a face and name appeared on the screen, he said, "That's what he looks like. Study him, kid, and memorize his face."

"Okay, well, I'll try." Lancelot stared at the man. "How can I memorize his face? He looks like everybody else!"

"Of course, he looks like everybody else. Agents are supposed to look like everybody else. That makes them harder to identify."

"You know, Mr. Biggs," he began in the most reasonable voice he was capable. "We can't possibly…"

Totally ignoring Lancelot, Mr. Biggs grabbed a phone off his desk, a miniature camera out of a drawer, and shoved a newspaper into Lancelot's middle section, which generated an oomph sound from the gaping decoder. Opening a closet door, he snatched a golf cap and a straw hat off a hook, hesitated a second then took a sport coat off a hangar and draped it over his shoulder.

Shooing Lancelot out of the way, Mr. Biggs locked up his office and the decoding room before striding with urgency and purpose through the backdoor with Lancelot staggering behind. Having made a quick call to Chief, he opened the door and slid behind the wheel of a rusted-out truck that would have been rejected by any respectable junkyard in town.

Lancelot gazed longingly at the backdoor of the agency remembering the mission he was on with Mr. Biggs four weeks ago. All he had to do then was walk along a dimly lit street, climb down a ladder into a tunnel, tap one of the bad guys on the shoulder with a broom handle, then scream his lungs out in the upstairs bathroom for ten minutes. This was altogether different. He might actually have to stop someone from handing over classified information to a foreign agent. He stood outside the truck in a state of anxiety until the head of security yelled, "Get in, kid! We've got no time to lose!"

Lancelot yanked on the passenger side door then used two hands, but it wouldn't budge.

"Sticks sometimes. Put some elbow grease into it, kid!"

Lancelot grabbed the handle tighter, planted his feet and tried again. It flew open, nearly knocking him over. He jumped inside and used both hands to close it, squeaking the entire way. If the plan included sneaking up on Firefly, they were toast and then some. He patted the seat beside him, then looked down and behind. "Where's the seatbelt?"

"We don't worry about sissy stuff like that around here."

"But what if we crash?!" Lancelot said, still searching just in case.

"Huh! Only crashed four times in my life and walked away without a scratch both times."

"'Both times'?"

"Well, hobbled a bit after two of the crashes."

"I see. Well, that's comforting—I guess," Lancelot said. "You know, Mr. Biggs, there's tons of statistics out there to prove that…"

"I know all about statistics, and I'm getting them first chance I get. Just haven't gotten around to it yet."

The truck started, backfired, and stalled out. Mr. Biggs jammed down on the gas pedal twice and the engine turned over. Putting the truck in reverse, they flew backward, then with an unsettling grinding noise, he shoved the knob into first gear, and they hopped out of the parking lot.

Lancelot looked at the seat covers torn in five places and a gaping hole on the floor between his feet. "How old is this, uh, truck?"

"No idea. We've been through a lot together. So long as it runs, that's all I care about." Four minutes later, Mr. Biggs glanced at Lancelot. "Call Chief and tell him we're five blocks away. ETA is forty-five seconds."

Lancelot picked up the cell phone, dropped it then picked it up again. "What's Chief's number?"

"Press one. It'll take you directly to him."

"Hello, Chief!" Lancelot shouted. "Oh, sorry, Chief. Our ETA is forty-five seconds," he said then listened carefully. "We follow this guy—I mean Firefly then take a picture of the handoff. The backup is on the way, and they'll make the arrest after he hands over the classified documents? Should we just take the photos and leave?" His shoulders sagged. "I see. Okay." He hung up and stared at the phone.

"We tail Firefly, maintain visual contact, take photos of the handoff, then backup will arrest them when they get here. But we've got to maintain our position until backup arrives. Now, put that phone on vibrate and stick it in your back pocket."

"How did you know that?"

"Standard procedure, kid."

They squealed around the corner with Lancelot grabbing hold of what was left of the dashboard then came to a skidding halt half a block from the Main Street Hotel. After the engine conked out, Lancelot felt lucky to be alive, but couldn't guarantee what the next thirty minutes held.

Mr. Biggs looked at his rearview mirror then his side mirror before checking his watch. "Fifteen minutes till sixteen hundred hours," he said in a low, measured voice.

Lancelot wiped his forehead then turned the knob at his elbow around twice, but the window didn't budge.

"It's broken."

"Your side broken, too?"

"No, it works."

"What if your truck slides into a lake? You'll get out but I'll drown."

The head of security looked into Lancelot's eyes. "You don't have to worry about that kind of thing, kid. I'll save you."

Lancelot's forehead smoothed out as he stared back at the head of security. "You would? You mean you really would save me?"

"I would."

"Thank you," Lancelot said softly.

Silence grew increasingly heavy and the interior of the truck increasingly hotter as they stared at the steps leading up to the Main Street Hotel.

Mr. Biggs tapped his fingertips on the steering wheel as he pressed his lips inward never taking his eyes off the door to the hotel. He donned the golf cap, picked up his sport coat then shoved open the door. "Hand me half of that newspaper, kid," he said softly.

"Where are you going?"

"A little reconnaissance trip," Mr. Biggs replied, barely moving his lips. "Need to know the layout of the hotel, where the exits are, who's in the lobby in case we need to go in there. Won't be more than a couple of minutes."

"What if Firefly shows up while you're gone?" Lancelot said trying desperately to maintain an even voice. "What am I supposed to do?"

"Don't worry about it, kid. Won't happen," Mr. Biggs said. "Be back in a few minutes."

As Mr. Biggs walked away from the truck, Lancelot observed a different side of him. He walked with his head held high never looking to the left or right as if the entire world revolved around him. How many faces and personalities did Mr. Biggs possess? He'd probably never know.

Lancelot's eyes darted down the street and across to the opposite sidewalk. Two men sat on a bench within the shade of an awning.

There were ordinary people strolling up and down the sidewalk with no idea a traitor was inside the hotel waiting to pass off classified information to the enemy.

What if Firefly used the back exit and Mr. Biggs didn't see him? Did he possess the inner resources to follow Firefly on his own? He didn't know how to follow someone. He'd be spotted for the total amateur he was within seconds.

The front door opened and Mr. Biggs stepped out. Instead of heading towards the truck, he turned the other way, rounded the corner, then reappeared carrying his sport coat and golf cap, and resumed his regular walk. Yet, he appeared oddly distracted rather than intensely focused as he was when he left.

When he slipped behind the wheel, Lancelot waited. but Mr. Biggs stared straight ahead. "What happened?"

Mr. Biggs glanced at Lancelot then gave his full attention to the hotel. "There are three exits on the main floor, two elevators down a hallway to the left. The Reservation Desk is to the right with one young woman working behind it. Two other people are sitting in the lobby looking at their laptops. Ten people in the coffee shop about ready to leave. No sign of Firefly."

"Didn't people think it was weird you were standing there counting everybody?"

Mr. Biggs raised an eyebrow. "The art of reconnaissance is subtly, kid. Nobody should know you're checking them out. Worst case scenario, you wouldn't be able to leave the place if they knew you were there to spy on them."

"Oh, I guess you're right."

"I need the phone, kid," Mr. Biggs said suddenly. "Bake? Any of the boys downtown close to the Main Street Hotel?" He listened then said, "Okay, might need backup. Not sure. Depends on when Chief gets here. Right, thanks, Bake."

Lancelot replaced the phone in his back pocket. "Was Mr. Baker the one I met a few weeks ago at the safehouse?" When Mr. Biggs nodded, he said, "Do we need extra backup?"

"Not sure. Something doesn't look right."

"Like what?

"Later, kid."

At exactly four o'clock, Firefly pressed through the door looking as ordinary in person as he did on the computer screen. He adjusted his tie as his eyes drifted aimlessly across the street. Reaching inside a breast pocket, he retrieved his sunglasses, then casually looked to the left before sliding them on. He trotted down the steps while his head pivoted to the right, then turned in their direction.

Mr. Biggs picked up the newspaper and shook it open in front of his face. "Lean down like you're checking your shoelaces, kid." He watched Firefly in his side mirror until he was forty feet beyond them then slid the camera into a side pocket and jammed the straw hat onto his head. He eased his door open, motioning for Lancelot to exit the truck through the driver's side. He nodded across the street where his eyes lingered a fraction of a second. "You follow him on that side, kid; I'll tail him on this side. Don't look at him and don't get too close. If he stops, step into a shop and keep watch through the window until he moves on. If he turns onto another street, turn with him but maintain your distance."

Lancelot nodded. He stumbled across the street to the sidewalk unaware that a man stood in the shadows only a few yards from him.

He'd seen the truck arrive and waited patiently knowing the appointed time was near. When the decoder reached the sidewalk, the man stepped outside the protection of the shadow and began to follow the followers. Disguised as a much older man leaning heavily on a cane, he fell under the radar screen of threat.

Two blocks later, Firefly drew up short and waited for the light to change. Lancelot stopped and struggled to remember what he was supposed to do. Mr. Biggs stepped inside a recessed area of a cafe, so Lancelot pressed through the nearest door.

The follower retreated to a nearby bench where he sat heavily wiping his brow with his shirt sleeve.

Firefly was on the move again, so Lancelot bolted through the door and edged along, keeping his eyes on the head of security rather than Firefly.

When the traitor stopped in front of a store window, Mr. Biggs stepped through a door and Lancelot rounded a corner into an alley then turned toward the brick wall, tapping nervously on the wall with his fingertips.

The follower slipped inside a café and ordered a coffee to go. He knew the final destination. Now he gave them time to get settled before he made his move.

Firefly adjusted his tie as he surveyed the area. Finally, he crossed the street and headed into the alley walking past Lancelot before entering a park at the first entrance.

Lancelot watched through glazed eyes as Firefly disappeared.

Mr. Biggs crossed the street at a trot, grabbed Lancelot's arm, and dragged him along. "See that second entrance over there?"

"Yes, I see it!"

"Amble," Mr. Biggs said. "Do you know what 'amble' means?"

"Amble? Yes, I know what amble means."

"Okay, call Chief first. Do you remember his number?"

"One?"

"That's right! Tell Chief our location then amble through that second entrance, locate Firefly then do not look at him again. Just watch him out of the corner of your eye. Got that!?"

Lancelot inhaled deeply. "Got it."

Mr. Biggs tore off his straw hat, pulled out the golf cap and drew it down over his forehead, then rolled up the straw hat, and shoved it in Lancelot's direction. "Put that in your back pocket, kid."

"Why are you changing hats?"

"People see hats before they see your face." Just before walking through the gate, the head of security checked over his shoulder. He stretched his arm towards the next entrance, then mouthed the word, "Go!"

Lancelot bolted to the second entrance, drew out the phone, then pressed Chief's number. "Chief? We're at the park off Main Street. There are two entrances. Firefly went through the first entrance and Mr. Biggs followed him. I'm at the second entrance and I'm supposed to go inside the park after I've called you."

There was a terrifying five seconds of silence while Lancelot waited for Chief's response. "We've had a delayed," he said.

"A-a what?" Lancelot stammered.

"Delay. Can't be helped. We're moving as fast as we can." And with that, Chief disconnected the call.

Delay? What did that mean? A couple of minutes? Twenty minutes? How long were they on their own? Straightening his shoulders, he entered the park, performing a truly inspired imitation of an amble. His eyes scanned the area and stopped for a fraction of a second as he spotted Firefly. His head faced forward while his eyes focused on the traitor. He was getting the hang of this tailing business—more or less as long as his legs didn't give out.

Suddenly, Firefly stopped at the side of a circular fountain with various paths leading into the center of the park.

Mr. Biggs and Lancelot took cover behind separate bushes, maintaining visual contact through slits in the shrubbery.

The follower slipped through the second entrance to the park then silently positioned himself thirty feet behind Lancelot. He observed the decoder then shifted his eyes to Firefly and the path the foreign agent would take to meet the intelligence agency's traitor.

Firefly casually turned in a circle. When his back was to them, the head of security leaped over three bushes and knelt beside Lancelot. "Did you reach Chief?" he whispered.

Lancelot swallowed. "There's been a delay."

"What's their ETA?"

"Chief didn't say. He hung up after telling me there was a delay." Perhaps they could amble out of the park and wait for the people who actually knew what they were doing, but that idea was squashed with Mr. Biggs' next sentence. "I need the phone." When Lancelot handed it to him, the head of security sent a text message. Lancelot tried to read it, but the phone was angled away from him.

Mr. Biggs returned the phone then whispered, "Do you know how to operate a camera?" When Lancelot nodded, Mr. Biggs handed the camera to him then said, "Wait till Firefly turns sideways then take several shots of him. If he turns to face you take several more. The most important photos you'll take are of the person he's here to meet and the handoff, so be ready for that."

"Why am I taking the photos?"

"I have other business to take care of."

Lancelot's eyes widened and he nearly forgot to whisper. "You're leaving?"

"We've got company."

"Company? What do you mean?"

"Somebody followed us from the hotel to the park."

Lancelot swallowed hard. "I didn't see anybody who looked suspicious."

"That's the idea, kid. They never look suspicious." Mr. Biggs glanced beyond Lancelot then said, "Did you see an old man walking behind you?"

Lancelot reviewed the people his anxious mind recorded then nodded. "But he used a cane. He was limping. You can't think he's..."

"He forgot to limp. Twice."

"Do you know where he is now?"

"Thirty feet in back of us," Mr. Biggs said, "I'm going to crawl between these two rows of bushes and get behind him. You stay here and take those photos."

Lancelot watched Mr. Biggs leave then lifted the camera to his right eye trying to still his trembling hands. When Firefly turned in a slow circle, Lancelot pressed the button, then pressed it repeatedly hoping to capture a decent photo of him.

Within minutes, another man arrived overplaying his role as a tourist. He wore a bright-colored shirt with a wide visor and sunglasses which hid his eyes. To add to his image, a cheap camera hung at the end of a strap draped around his neck.

Even from Lancelot's vantagepoint, he caught Firefly's look of disdain. That glance spoke volumes of the insult Firefly felt at having a new recruit sent for this assignment. He carried vital, top-classified information and they sent somebody fresh out of training. Firefly altered his position taking in the thickness of the raw recruit's side pocket where the transfer of money awaited.

The men stood ten feet apart totally ignoring each other while looking at a forty-degree angle in Lancelot's direction. Pressing the bushes aside, he lifted the camera and started shooting photos.

The foreign agent made his way to the beginning of the line of rose bushes leaning over to inhale their fragrance. Firefly lifted his wrist and looked pointedly at his watch, uttered a sigh as if he'd lost track of time, then quickly headed for the path which led out of the park. He tripped quite convincingly, reached inside an inner pocket while the other man withdrew a thick envelope. Once the handoff was executed, both men turned in opposite directions and picked up a steady but rapid pace.

They were getting away and Lancelot look desperately over his shoulder.

Suddenly, Mr. Biggs stood at his side. His eyes tracked the direction the foreign agent was taking then shot forward and intercepted him hallway to the park's first exit With thirty years of army experience behind him, Mr. Biggs caught the agent off balance, and he crashed to the ground. The raw recruit hit the sidewalk; the breath completely knocked out of him.

Mr. Biggs reached inside the man's pocket and took possession of the classified documents then shoved them inside his shirt. He kept his weight centered on the top part of the man's body, so it was impossible for the struggling man to get to his feet.

This only happened in movies and Lancelot was having difficulty transferring what he saw on the screen to the real-time performance unfolding in front of his eyes.

"Don't just stand there!" Mr. Biggs shouted as he nodded to Firefly, who backed up and ran to the first exit. "Get him!"

Lancelot ran to the second exit, looked around the corner, and stepped back. He wasn't good enough to make the middle school soccer team, so how was he supposed to stop this guy?!

Firefly took one last look inside the park then broke into a run, heading in Lancelot's direction. As Firefly was about to pass the second exit, Lancelot threw himself on the ground directly in the escapee's pathway. Firefly flailed trying to keep his balance, but then Lancelot gave him an encouraging shove which flattened him to the ground. Lancelot scrambled to his hands and knees, then sat down on Firefly's legs. Actually, it was total overkill at this point because the agent was nearly unconscious.

Several minutes later, two cars wheeled around the corner, coming to a skidding halt several feet from where Lancelot had the agent under control.

Chief signaled two men to take charge of Firefly then helped Lancelot to his shaky feet. "Well, done," he said, attempting to keep the surprise out of his voice. "Where's Goliath?"

"Goliath?" Lancelot asked in a thin voice, yet he'd heard Kat call him Goliath at the safehouse.

"Yes," Chief said then drew back quickly. "I mean where's Biggs?"

"He's inside the park," Lancelot said as he looked oddly at Chief.

With surprising speed, Chief led two other agents into the park followed by Lancelot at a halting pace. He collapsed on a nearby bench as Mr. Biggs stood and the Chief's men hauled the foreign agent to his feet then exited the park.

The head of security handed Chief the classified documents, which he slid into an inside pocket.

"Good work, Goliath," Chief said in a low voice then leaned in like two old buddies having a conversation at a baseball game. He listened as Goliath briefed him concerning the events that took place in the last thirty minutes.

"You saw someone follow you from the hotel?" Chief said.

"Yes, he was in place across the street from the hotel when we got there," Mr. Biggs said. "Didn't look right. Caried a cane but forgot to limp."

Chief nodded. "That's when you called Bake."

"Right. Couple of the boys were nearby. They've got him."

"Good work, Goliath," Chief said. "Emergencies are always tough."

There was that name again—like a code name. Lancelot stared at the head of security and wondered. Army Intelligence. Goliath. Was that his code name?

It was a quiet trip back to the intelligence agency, except Mr. Biggs hummed and tapped a beat on his steering wheel.

Lancelot shifted his weight as he glanced at the head of security. The truck rounded the corner into the parking lot then stalled out with only enough momentum to coast into a parking spot.

"Probably needs a tune-up," Mr. Biggs said as he headed into the building. He stopped in front of the decoding room and unlocked the door.

"I was just wondering," Lancelot said.

"Wondering what?"

"Why did Chief and Kat call you Goliath?"

"Private joke, kid, that's all." Mr. Biggs shifted his weight. "Around here, you can get sucked under if you're not careful. You know what I mean?" he said, eyeing the boy. When Lancelot nodded, he walked down the hallway to his room, unlocked the door, then looked at Lancelot. "Good work, kid."

The tiniest of smiles creased Lancelot's lips. "Thanks, Mr. Biggs."

He sat down at his desk, rotated his shoulders, and laid the next three coded messages on his desk. His hands still trembled slightly, but inside, a strange sort of warmth settled in.

The Missing Witness
Chapter 1

Within three hours of her plane landing, Katherine Stephens came to a frightening conclusion. The two men assigned to protect her had actually imprisoned her. She didn't realize she was a prisoner until she decided to take a walk an hour after they arrived at the safehouse.

The doors leading to the outside were locked and bolted. Kat realized there had been a shift when she was denied access to the key and refused to be accompanied on the walk. Being well trained as an intelligence officer, she reacted calmly to the situation.

She'd spent her entire adult life in army intelligence with Colonel Biggs then followed him to the intelligence agency when they both retired. He accepted a position as head of security, but most people at the agency knew he was a great deal more than that even though that was his official title.

Kat spent several years working out of the intelligence agency's central office, then was reassigned to a series of foreign embassies. Wearing a mask to hide her true feelings came naturally.

The two men had taken her suitcase as soon as they arrived at the safehouse and returned it to her room shortly afterwards. Once they left her room, she opened it. The tiniest of smiles creased her lips. They had replaced the items in her suitcase almost perfectly. Only two small objects were out of place. She closed the suitcase and placed it in the closet.

Sitting on a rocking chair, she soothed herself by rocking slowly back and forth. It hadn't mattered that they'd taken her suitcase. Nothing of any importance was in there. What they searched for was tucked away in a tiny insert on the inside of her shoe. It was a bit of an inconvenience having it in that position, but if her shoes were checked, they'd expect to find something in the heel of the shoe.

That evening, one of them prepared a soothing cup of tea before she went to bed. But her dreams were unsettling that night. A soft, calming voice explained that it had all been a misunderstanding. There was no leak of classified information at the embassy where she'd been assigned. No, just a series of careless mistakes by a new employee with no intent to betray their country.

Kat awoke the next morning doubting herself for the first time in her career as an intelligence officer. She sat on the window seat in her bedroom drawing the curtains closed so she was hidden from view to anyone entering her room. She needed solitude and time to review what had happened over the past few weeks. While she thought, she gazed at the tall fence that surrounded the safehouse. Had she been wrong about the person she considered a traitor?

She was assigned to a foreign embassy in the section devoted to developing trade between the two countries. In reality, she was part of an intelligence team gathering information critical to the interest and security of her country. It was a small group of people who had known and trusted each other for some time.

As is often the case, something didn't feel quite right. Something was out of place just enough to create doubt. Then she overheard a conversation and knew there'd been a leak of classified information available to only a few. The leak had to come from her small department and the information was given to a country with whom relations were already stretched to the breaking point.

The problem was she didn't know the source of the leak. Who was guilty? There wasn't enough evidence to report it to her immediate supervisor or officials at headquarters, so she set a trap. They were individual traps so she'd know in an instant which person had betrayed them. Within days of setting the trap, the traitor was revealed.

Kat attended an embassy function where people stood in groups of twos and threes chatting. She stood off to the side, a camera hidden in her purse ready to snap an incriminating photo if it came to that. She scanned the groups hoping what she feared wouldn't happen.

Two people caught her eye as they drifted to the edge of the room. The exchange was done so subtly that Kat only had two seconds to take photos. Why had they chosen a time when many people could witness their exchange. Perhaps it was safer to meet where many people were gathered rather than risk meeting alone where it would arouse suspicion if anyone saw them.

After the embassy closed for the day, Kat made her way from her office to the lab where she converted the images into microfilm. She wasn't sure why she felt the need for a backup of the photos on the camera. But where there was one traitor, there may be more.

The following morning, Kat met her immediate superior and explained the situation. Before she left, he asked for the camera she'd used and wanted to know if they were the only photos she'd taken. She assured him that they were the only photos she'd taken. She wasn't sure why she neglected to tell him about the microfilm.

Late that afternoon, officials at headquarters arranged for her to fly home. They wanted a full report. Someone would pick her up at the airport and drive her to a secure location. During the flight, Kat pondered the fact that it didn't take long for her immediate superior to contact headquarters. She'd been called home. But why hadn't an internal investigation been conducted? She'd discover what they planned to do about this breach of security when she met with them.

It was time for breakfast. Kat cast another glance at the backyard of the safehouse, pushed the curtains aside, and left the security of the window seat. But when she stood up, she felt dizzy. It wasn't the type of dizziness where she feared falling. It was just enough that she held onto the rail on her way down the steps.

It must be the jet lag from flying through seven time zones to reach her destination. She sat at the table sipping her tea while her eyes blinked as she attempted to bring the men's faces into focus. The two men made light conversation. Was it her imagination or did their eyes linger on her face just a little longer than normal?

Throughout breakfast, her thinking was muddled as if everything functioned in slow motion. When the men spoke to her, she watched their lips move in a delayed reaction. Like an old movie, the movement of their lips was out of sync with the sound of their voice. Kat closed her eyes tightly, but when she opened them again, everything was still off.

Something else was puzzling. They smiled but their actions were out of alignment with what was happening. Even though her thinking was hazy, Kat realized escape was the only solution. She had to know whether she had been mistaken about the traitor. Because, if there was a traitor at the embassy then her immediate superior was part of the conspiracy and had planned for her to disappear.

She could almost hear her immediate superior at the embassy assuring everyone she was on vacation for a couple of weeks. How easy it would be to tell her colleagues there had been a tragic accident. Kat couldn't sit back and allow that "tragic accident" to occur. She had to pull herself together and think.

They suggested a very light sleeping pill would give her a more restful sleep. They made a joke of inspecting the interior of her mouth to make sure she'd swallowed it and laughed merrily as they patted her on the shoulder.

The following morning, they decided she looked a little tired. Perhaps, it would be better if she remained in her room and rested. They would be more than happy to prepare a tray for her meals and deliver them to her room. An hour before lunchtime, her muddled thinking slowly realized they were drugging her. They put something in what she ate or drank so she conducted an experiment. At lunch, Kat ate the food but dumped the water down the sink adjoining her bedroom. Two hours later, her clarity of thinking was nearly normal.

They checked on her every two hours. She played the part of a woman in a drugged state of mind. But, apparently the act wasn't good enough.

At six o'clock, one of the men walked through the door with her dinner tray. After he left, she took the glass and dumped its contents down the sink then ate the food. Within thirty minutes, her vision was blurred again. She pressed her hand against her forehead willing her mind to overcome this nightmare.

That night, the other man handed her a sleeping pill then checked the interior of her mouth to make sure she'd swallowed it. After he left, she took the sleeping pill out of her mouth and placed it inside her pocket beside the first one. She saved the sleeping pills both nights. Even through the haze, the experienced intelligence officer understood something as fundamental as hiding a pill inside her mouth while seeming to swallow it. Those two men were thugs not trained agents.

What made it infinitely easier was when the guard stood over her with the nightly sleeping pill, she smelled alcohol on his breath. They were a sloppy lot. They were careless about taking her meal trays back to the kitchen, too.

With a hand that was far from steady, she placed her sleeping pills on one spoon then used another spoon to crush them. She dumped the crushed pills into a glass, added a small amount of water, and stirred till the sleeping pills were dissolved. Setting it aside, she sat in her rocking chair and slowly rocked.

One of the men had stepped out the night before and hadn't returned for hours. If luck smiled on her, the same would happen tonight.

Being confident that she had swallowed the sleeping pills, they hadn't bothered locking her bedroom door. Quietly, she opened it an inch and listened. When she heard the backdoor close, she knew one of them had left.

Kat waited until the remaining guard stumble into the kitchen to pick up a snack. She removed her shoes, slipped out of her room, then slowly descended the stairway with one hand enclosing the glass and the other one grasping the rail. Midway, she felt dizzy and sat down a few seconds. At the bottom step, she paused, then stepped across the hallway, and dumped the contents of her small glass into his drink.

When she heard him open the kitchen door, she made her way up the steps, closed the door, and leaned against it trying to catch her breath. It wasn't the exertion that created the shortness of breath, it was knowing this may be her only chance to escape. If they caught her, they'd lock her in her room with no chance of escape.

She slipped on her shoes and waited. Twenty minutes later, she retraced her steps. The television was blaring and he sat in a high-back chair with his back to her. Her singular thought was what if he hadn't finished his drink? Peering around the corner, she inched along the edge of the room keeping her eyes pinned to his chair. His hand lay limply over the side of the chair. His head lay on his chest. Had he failed to finish the drink and was merely dozing?

She placed her hand on his arm but he remained still. Grasping the house keys on the table beside him, she raced for the kitchen, unlocked the door, and slipped into the night.

Chapter 2

It was quiet on the ground floor of the intelligence agency when the front door buzzer sounded.

Mr. Biggs crossed the hall and entered the code to open the door.

From the decoding room partway down the hall, Lancelot peered around the corner. Not many people showed up at the intelligence agency this time of day. At first glance, he figured they were probably from headquarters. They wore dark suits and serious expressions. Obviously, Mr. Biggs didn't expect them to stay long, because he held the door open anticipating they wouldn't stay more than a few seconds.

The taller one opened his wallet containing his ID card. "Al Franklin."

The shorter, heavier one flipped open his wallet. "Ted Bernhardt."

"I see," Mr. Biggs said, taking a closer look at their ID cards without seeming to. "What can I do for you, boys?"

No one from headquarters had graced the entranced to the

intelligence agency in the time Lancelot had worked there. Why were they here now?

"We've come to discuss a matter of great importance," Franklin said. "Rather urgent."

"Look, Chief's in a meeting right now, so you'll have to come back later," Mr. Biggs said.

"We didn't come to see your chief," Bernhardt said. "We came to see you."

"Me?"

"We're here to discuss somebody you know," Bernhardt said.

Mr. Biggs still held the door open waiting for them to leave. "Like who?"

"Katherine Stephens," Franklin said. "Something's happened to her."

"Kat?" Mr. Biggs said, his face paled but that was the only outward sign that the information came as a shock. When the agents nodded, he let the door slide off his fingers then led the men into his office. Agent Franklin gave the door a careless shove and it failed to close by two inches.

Lancelot had only spoken with Kat for a moment at the safehouse but he liked her. He silently inched forward then stood quietly outside Mr. Biggs' door.

"Okay. What's happened to her?" Mr. Biggs said.

"We felt Katherine Stephens had been working too hard. She hasn't felt well for a while and we flew her back for evaluation," Al Franklin said. "But she's missing. We don't know where she is or what her condition is."

"We decided to contact you since you're old friends," Bernhardt said.

"What do you mean she hasn't felt well from working too hard? She's always worked too hard," Mr. Biggs said with an edge to his voice. "What happened?"

"She's an intelligence officer in one of our embassies," Ted Bernhardt said. "Rather not say which country. Ms. Stephens hasn't been acting herself. She started making wild claims about her associates, so the decision was made to bring her back for a checkup."

"What sort of wild claims?"

"Well, she claims there were leaks of classified information within the embassy," Franklin said. "A thorough investigation took place. Her claims are totally unfounded."

"Somebody gave information to a country not too friendly to ours. Is that it?" Mr. Biggs said, but only someone who knew him heard the sarcasm in his voice.

Al Franklin shifted uncomfortably in his chair. "That's about it. When she reported it, we immediately conducted a thorough investigation. Strictly below the radar screen, you understand. Only the department head knew about the investigation."

"If these allegations continued, we were concerned that her safety may be in jeopardy. So we flew her back to the states and placed her in one of our safehouses," Franklin said. "We made an appointment for an evaluation. Have two men on duty round the clock to keep an eye on her. Then one night, her sleeping pills ended up in one of the men's drink and he was out for twelve hours. When he woke up, she was gone."

"How do you think the sleeping pills ended up in his drink?" Mr.

Biggs' said in a tight voice. He wanted to ask why Kat was given sleeping pills but he had a good idea why.

The men exchanged glances again and cleared their throats while they decided how to spin this.

"For a short time that night, there was only one person on duty with Ms. Stephens. The other one had stepped out for an hour or so. Needed fresh air, I suspect," Bernhardt said knowing it was a lame excuse. "Ms. Stephens had been experiencing difficulty sleeping for some time even at the embassy where she'd been assigned. He saw her put the sleeping pill in her mouth, she must have shoved the pill to the side and didn't swallow it."

"Oldest trick in the books," Mr. Biggs said, knowing what they said was far from the truth. He was relieved that Kat had escaped because he knew without a doubt the person was not on duty to protect her. He was on duty to make sure she didn't leave. "Kat saved her sleeping pills then somehow slipped them into his drink. Is that what you think?"

"Yes, that's about it," Franklin said.

Again, there was silence while the two men shifted in their chairs.

"When did this happen?" Mr. Biggs said.

"Two nights ago," Franklin said.

"Two nights ago!" Mr. Biggs said. "You won't find her now. Why did you wait so long to contact me?"

"Yes. Well," Bernhardt said. "That's why we're here now."

"What do you expect me to do?" Mr. Biggs said.

"It's not easy to track her down when there's nothing to go on," Bernhardt said. "We're concerned that certain people may have staked out the safehouse, saw her slip away, then grabbed her."

"There's always that possibility. But where do I fit into this?"

"You knew her," Bernhardt said. "The people she accused may not have her which means she's on the run. We figured you might have an idea where she might be hiding. Naturally, our main concern is her mental instability and safety."

"Naturally," Mr. Biggs repeated, with a touch more sarcasm. "Why didn't you come to me right away?"

"We didn't want to bring in her old army intelligence friends," Al Franklin said. "After all, that was ten years ago."

"We're reaching out to you now before something unfortunate happens to her," Bernhardt said. "Any information you can give us might save her life."

"Yes, well, I'm interested in saving her life, too," Mr. Biggs said.

Lancelot could hear rather than see Mr. Biggs' irritation. He also knew he was staring at the floor stalling for time so that his final answer appeared logical.

"Have to think about it, boys," Mr. Biggs finally said.

Good answer Lancelot thought. Didn't offend the two officials from headquarters but put the answer on hold for a while.

"Fair enough," Franklin said. "You'll get back to us after you've had time to think about it."

"I'll get back to you if something turns up," Mr. Biggs said, not committing himself to an agreement.

"Here's my card," Ted Bernhardt said. "Call me at the number I've written on the back. It's my direct line, so you won't have to go through anyone else to reach me."

Lancelot tiptoed back to his office and sat at his desk then picked up a coded message he'd been working on earlier in the morning. But at the back of his mind he could not believe Kat had some type of mental breakdown. So why was she hiding? And who was she hiding from? And why didn't Mr. Biggs tell them he'd seen her very recently?

Chapter 3

Kat glanced over her shoulder as she increased the distance from the house where she'd been kept a prisoner. When dizziness overtook her, she stepped inside a recessed doorway and leaned against it, keeping within the shadows rendering her invisible to anyone passing by. Even though the streets were empty, anyone looking out a window would immediately become suspicious of someone staggering down the street or sitting on the curb.

She closed her eyes then opened them. Everything was still viewed in doubles. There were two streetlights instead of one, two stop signs instead of one. Kat inhaled deeply to keep from being overcome with nausea.

She maintained a slow but steady pace. Her fingertips glided across the surface of the buildings to maintain her balance. Kat replayed crushing her sleeping pills and pouring them into the man's drink. Even with everything at stake, her mouth formed a brief smile.

Six blocks later, she heard running footsteps behind her. She slipped inside the shelter of another recessed doorway, pressed her body against the wall, then waited and listened.

The pounding footsteps drew nearer. There would only be a fraction of a second to identify whether it was the other man. Had he returned early and tried to awaken his partner? The previous night he hadn't returned for hours.

She held her breath as he raced by, but Kat wasn't sure. This man wore a coat and hat. It was dark. She waited until there was complete silence then reversed direction and turned at the intersection.

Perhaps good fortune would smile on her, and she'd have the rest of the night to make her way to a safehouse. But where was the closest one? She had only a vague idea where she was and it wasn't near any of the safehouses maintained by the intelligence agency. At least none that she knew about. On foot, was the only way she could get there.

She had no money and no phone. They'd taken both. She'd heard nerve wracking stories of other agents who'd been in similar situations. But she'd never been on the run herself.

Two hours later after a dozen twists and turns through alleys, she slowly climbed the steps to a familiar safehouse using both hands on the rail to pull herself along. She and Goliath had used this house before. She needed to contact him but with no phone she couldn't call him. With no money, she couldn't take a taxi or any other means of transportation. She'd trust Goliath with her life. But her mind and body needed to recover and regain equilibrium.

There was a pad with a code attached to the lock. She leaned against the door as she willed her head to stop spinning. Sixty desperate seconds later, she remembered the code, entered it, turned the knob, and stepped inside. Immediately, she bolted it shut so no one could get in through the front door.

It was a rowhouse with houses butting up against it on both sides, so there were only two doors, the front and the backdoor. Kat made her way past the stairs leading to the second floor then through the dining room and into the kitchen. She looked through the window memorizing what cars were in the alley, bolted the door, and dropped onto a kitchen chair.

There was always a supply of unperishable food in the safehouse, so there were cans of food in the cupboard and frozen items in the freezer. But when she searched through the cupboards and freezer, she found very few items. She had no money and not much to eat. What Kat needed more than anything was a hot, soothing cup of tea. Using the top of the table to push herself up from the chair, she boiled water, brewed the tea then sat and sipped it while she thought. Her normally organized mind accustomed to thinking strategically was numb. She needed sleep. Would the drug wear off completely by the morning?

Finished with her tea, she retraced her steps to the front of the house. There were four small bedrooms to choose from. She chose the one in the back then bolted the bedroom door shut. With no energy left, she allowed her body to drop onto the bed then lifted her legs over the edge and drew them into a fetal position. Pulling the side of the quilt over herself, she fell into an uneasy sleep.

There was no soothing voice that night telling her it had all been a misunderstanding. There was no leak of classified information at the embassy. No voice telling her it was just a series of careless mistakes by a new employee with no intent to betray their country.

The following day, she opened her eyes, then drew her brows together and blinked. Her memory slowly returned and she knew where she was and why she was here. Her eyes drifted to the closet door. She threw back the quilt and stood on legs that felt stronger, not perfect but a definite improvement.

Kat opened the closet door and contemplated what type of disguise she needed. There were clothes of every size and style along with wigs, fake beards, and mustaches. Kat was tall and slender with medium length light brown hair. She could easily disguise herself as either gender. She chose a wig with streaks of gray in it, a long, shapeless dress that contained internal padding which added thirty pounds to her body, then laid them on a chair. She'd take care of the makeup just before she left that evening. There were several canes leaning against the corner. They were great props. They were also good weapons.

Having made that decision, she headed for the kitchen where she found half a loaf of bread in the freezer. While the tea was brewing, she toasted two pieces. Again, she sipped and thought. When nightfall came, she changed into the clothes she'd chosen that morning, applied makeup to age her face then grabbed one of the canes. She shut off the kitchen light then peeked through the heavy curtains at the backdoor window to check for movement.

When all appeared still and quiet, she left and kept to the side of the alley as she walked two blocks to the nearest café. She peered through the edge of the window. She was in luck. It was a busy night. The servers were walking rapidly between the tables and the kitchen. The customers were absorbed with each other. She searched for a small corner table with one person. There was a single person who rose and left for a moment leaving his phone on the table.

Kat slipped through the door then hunched over leaning on her cane as she made her way to the table. She sat down, casually looked around then slid the phone inside her pocket. She headed for the back of the café where the restrooms and a backdoor were located. People were too preoccupied to notice that an old woman had left so suddenly.

She chose an alternate route on her return trip then waited behind a shrub at the beginning of her alley until she was reasonably confident she hadn't been followed and no one was waiting for her.

Kat entered the code to unlock the backdoor, bolted it then walked directly through to the front of the house. She was exhausted. She'd call Goliath after she locked herself inside her bedroom. She was halfway up the stairs when she heard someone entering the code to unlock the front door. Was it someone she knew or had there been a break in security so someone had access to the codes to enter the safehouses. She heard the door unlock, but she'd bolted the door from the inside, so no one could enter. There was a light tap on the front door. Slowly, she descended the stairs and cautiously peered through a side window.

Chapter 4

Mr. Biggs entered the code that allowed the front door to swing open then mumbled a few departing words to Agents Bernhard and Franklin. His footsteps echoed down the hallway then stopped at Lancelot's doorway.

Lancelot's eyes stared unseeing at a message that was only partially decoded. He pushed up glasses to see the image more clearly.

"You always decode messages upside down?"

Lancelot focused on the paper he held then slowly turned it right side up. "Well, uh, I was…" His face turned the slightest shade of pink. He was only a tiny bit embarrassed. After all, they'd been on several missions together so they didn't have many secrets, at least on Lancelot's side of the equation. Mr. Biggs never gave anything away. He was a mystery Lancelot would never figure out, nor would anyone else.

Mr. Biggs crossed the room and sat at the nighttime decoder's desk. In one hand, he carried his phone. In the other hand, he held Bernhardt's and Franklin's business cards by their edges which he carefully transferred to the desk.

Lancelot watched in fascination. The head of security had never sat at the other desk since the young decoder had been employed at the agency. And why did Mr. Biggs carry the cards by their edges? Fingerprints?

The muscles of Mr. Biggs face tightened as he made a call. "Ed? Biggs here," he said then hesitated. "Look, Ed, two of your boys were here just now but something doesn't feel quite right. Need to know anything you can tell me about them." He gave Ed their names then shifted his attention to the mechanical pencils on the desk.

While Mr. Biggs waited, Lancelot wondered why he was in the decoding room making phone calls. Why not use his phone in the security office?

"Yes, I'm here," Mr. Biggs said. "What have you got?" The hand fiddling with the pencils froze over the desk as the furrows on his brow deepened. "I see. Okay. One more question, Ed. Do you know if Kat, I mean Katherine Stephens was suddenly ordered back to the states? Okay, I'll wait till you check."

Mr. Biggs rearranged the mechanical pencils several more times while he waited. "Yes, I'm still here," he said. "Kat's still at the embassy as far as you know? Well, those two imposters told me she was having mental health issues and was being held in a local safehouse until she could be evaluated. They said she left two nights ago and wondered if I had any information I could give them concerning her whereabouts. I don't know what's going on here. But if you say Kat's still at the embassy then that's all I need to know. Thanks, Ed."

"What's wrong?" Lancelot said.

Ignoring the question, Mr. Biggs rose from his chair. "Basement, kid. Got some sweeping to do."

"Sweeping? People come in at night to do that. Why do we need to sweep?"

"You'll see," Mr. Biggs said. He hurried down the basement steps with Lancelot close behind then walked directly to a shelf located on the far right. He pocketed a round device then rapidly retraced his steps.

"What did you stick in your pocket?"

"Checks for bugs planted. Listening devices," Mr. Biggs said

"You think those guys planted a bug in your office to listen in on your conversations?"

"Don't know. We'll find out."

"Ed at headquarters is sure those two guys are fakes," Lancelot said.

"Ed is head of human resources. He has access to the names of everyone who currently or has ever been employed by the agency. There's no record of them."

"Who are they then?"

"Probably the bad guys Kat's running away from."

"You think those two guys lied about Kat and there really is a security leak?" Lancelot said. "And they're looking for Kat to shut her up?"

"That's what I think."

"So, they came here hoping you knew where she was. What made them think you'd believe them? What made them think you wouldn't check up on them?"

"You'd be surprised how many people wouldn't call headquarters to check them out."

"But, why did you suspect them in the first place?"

"The print on their business cards is off just a fraction," Mr. Biggs said. "I had to look at it twice to see it, but it was there."

"That was sloppy of them."

"It was a rush job and somebody wasn't careful."

"But Ed is sure she's still at the embassy," Lancelot said.

"That's what he said. He's been at the agency so long he knows everything about everyone. So if Ed says Kat should still be at the embassy, then she should be there."

"But you think she's not at the embassy and you're worried about her."

"Right, I don't think she's there and I'm worried about her." Mr. Biggs took the stairs two-at-a-time and kept up a rapid pace down the hallway then said, "If Kat left the embassy, she had to tell someone she trusted where she was going and why."

"So there's at least two people involved in the leak at that embassy. The person who actually leaked the information and the person she told about it who she thought she could trust."

"Yes, at least two people are in on the conspiracy."

"How does that little gadget tell you those guys planted a bug in your office?"

"Light flickers if there's a listening device or something electronic," Mr. Biggs said then lifted his finger to his lips as they stood outside his office.

Seconds after entering the office, a light flashed within the small device. Mr. Biggs squatted down then signaled for Lancelot to follow suit. There it was. A tiny object was nestled in the shadow of the desk's overhang. They left and returned to the decoding room where Mr. Biggs closed the door.

Mr. Biggs sat on the edge of the nighttime decoder's chair then said, "How much did you hear of my conversation with those two men?"

Lancelot dropped his eyes. "What makes you think I heard anything?"

Mr. Biggs raised an eyebrow. "So how much?"

"Well." Lancelot swallowed. "Kat, Katherine Stephens, is an intelligence officer at an embassy in some country they wouldn't mention. She claims that someone is leaking classified information to some people who don't like us too much."

"And?"

"They claim there is no leak and Kat is suffering from nervous exhaustion or whatever they call it. They flew her back home. Something must have frightened her because she saved sleeping pills to put one of the men to sleep then disappeared in the middle of the night. They're trying to find her. That's why those two guys were just here."

"Yes," Mr. Biggs said softly. "They're trying to find Cracker Jack."

"What are we going to do?"

"I don't know because we have no idea where she is."

Chapter 5

Kat heard a knock on the front door then slowly descended the steps. She peeked through a slit in the curtain and saw a car parked by the curb that hadn't been there before. She shifted her focus from the car to the man standing in front of the door. The only source of light was a streetlight fifty feet away which created a dim outline of him, so it took Kat a moment to recognize who it was. Quickly she unbolted the door and threw it open. "Samson," she said, relief flooding her voice.

A man of average height, weight and looks wearing gray slacks and a polo shirt walked through the door. Samson's description fit much of the male population which increased his value as an agent.

'How did you know I was here?" Kat asked.

The man stared at her then said, "Who are you?"

For the first time in over a week, Kat chuckled. With the disguise she'd used to snatch the phone at the café, she was virtually unrecogniz-able. "Katherine Stephens."

"Cracker Jack? Why are you dressed like that?"

"Why am I dressed like this? It's a long story," Kat said then repeated her question. "How did you know I was here."

"I didn't," Samson said as he bolted the door again. "My plane landed but my luggage is stuck in another city. I had fifty dollars left after I paid to get my car out of the parking lot and put gas in it. I packed my credit cards in my suitcase. Stupid, I know. I was in a hurry to leave, so I threw everything into my suitcase and caught the next plane back."

"So you don't have money to stay anywhere."

"Right," Samson said. "No money. I decided to stay in one of the safehouses for a day or two until they find my suitcase. Is there food to eat? I'm starving!"

"I hope you like canned soup," Kat said then led the way to the kitchen. She warmed up the soup while Samson made tea for both of them.

While they sipped their tea, Samson said, "What are you doing here anyway?"

Kat sighed as she considered how much to reveal of what was happening. "There's a security leak at the embassy where I'm assigned. When I told my superior, someone called from headquarters ordering me home to make a full report. At the airport, two thugs posing as my guardians picked me up. I soon learned I was a prisoner. Headquarters knows nothing about me being here."

Samson shook his head. "How long have you been here?"

"Since about three o'clock last night."

"Does anyone know you're here?"

"No," Kat said, draining the last of her tea. "They took my money and my phone. I just got back from borrowing someone's phone at a café which is why I'm dressed like this. I need to call Goliath. He needs to take me to a safer place till we can figure out what to do."

"Biggs," Samson said. "Do you really think you can trust anyone right now? Even someone we used to work with in army intelligence? It's been at least ten years since I've seen any of them. Wouldn't it be better to hold off contacting someone till you know who you can trust?" He sat back in his chair then said. "Have you used your phone yet?"

"No. I was ready to make the call when you knocked on the door," she said, unsure why she didn't reveal that she'd seen Goliath fairly recently.

"Look, Kat. The problem is obvious. Once the person you borrowed the phone from finds out it's missing, he'll trace where it is and someone may come looking for you. We can use my phone till we develop a plan."

Kat understood her phone could be traced and it was an unnecessary risk now that Samson was here. "I understand."

"I'll get rid of it for you, okay? Be back in fifteen minutes at the most." Samson said then held out his hand. As soon as Kat gave him the phone, he turned off the kitchen light and parted the curtain. "Looks clear," he said. "Bolt the door after I leave. At least there are only two entrances to this safehouse. Makes security easier to maintain."

Kat bolted the door after Samson left then was struck by what he just said. 'At least there are only two entrances to this safehouse.' He'd forgotten. Or was he never briefed on the other two entrances? One of them was through the tunnel in the garage across the alley. She'd have used it but she didn't have the key to unlock the garage door.

She paced the distance between the dining and living rooms while she considered whether or not to tell him. At some point, that line of thinking was exchanged for why she was debating whether or not he should know. His behavior seemed absolutely normal. She'd known and trusted Samson for years. So why the hesitation?

The debate raged on in her mind until she heard a slight tap on the backdoor. After checking through the curtain, she unbolted the door, and Samson stepped through.

He sat at the kitchen table, his eyes studying the design on the tablecloth.

"Anything wrong?" Kat said.

Samson glanced up then his eyes returned to the tabletop. "No, just thinking about what supplies we need to keep us going for a day or two. We can't buy much for under fifty bucks, but we don't need much either." He rose from his chair and said, "I'm going to make a cup of chamomile tea then head upstairs. Want some?"

"Thanks, it'll help me to sleep. Been a rough stretch."

"Right. Been a rough stretch for both of us."

"What do you mean?" Kat said.

Samson shrugged his shoulders. "Nothing really. Just trying to sort through a few decisions."

They sipped in silence for the next fifteen minutes while Kat pondered what decisions Samson was working through. Wearily, they climbed the steps, utterly drained and in need of sleep.

Kat awoke the following morning dizzy and filled with doubt once again. The calm soothing voice had returned telling her it had all been a misunderstanding. There was no leak of classified information at the embassy where she'd been assigned. No, just a series of careless mistakes by a new employee with no intent to betray their country.

Samson was drinking coffee in the kitchen but looked up when Kat walked into the room. "You don't look too good, Cracker Jack. You feeling all right?"

Kat tried to focus on Samson, but he had two faces and she wasn't sure which one was actually his. "I'm all right."

"Sit down. I know how you like your tea and toast. It'll only take a few minutes. Then I'll head out to buy our few meager supplies since that's all we can afford."

Kat sat with her eyes following Samson as he moved around the kitchen. His image was narrowing into one form, but he remain distorted.

Samson set her tea and toast before her then watched as she consumed them. Partway through, he asked her again how she felt.

Kat slowly lifted her head and assured him she felt fine.

Samson observed her in silence as she ate breakfast then washed the dishes and put them away. He checked the short grocery list occasionally glancing at Kat. He peeked through a crack in the curtains into the back alley. The coast was clear, so he unbolted the door. "Be back in twenty minutes. Bolt the door after I leave. Okay?"

"Right." Kat's voice slurred. "You'll be back in twenty minutes." Twenty minutes went   by then thirty minutes then an hour. Like the night before, she paced between the dining and living rooms. Except this time, she staggered more than walked. He'd been gone too long.

Something was wrong.

Kat sat at the kitchen table with her elbows on the table, her head in her hands trying to see through the haze and lingering dizziness. Had he deserted her or was it something else?

She needed help from the person she had originally intended to call. It was broad daylight and the disguise she'd used at the café wouldn't work. She stumbled up the stairs and stood in front of her bedroom closet. People remembered hair color, height, and build. A wig to change her hair, a lightly padded coat to add weight, and shoes that added two inches to her height. She checked her appearance in a full-length mirror. Her thinking was still muddled but her vision was improving. She no longer saw two people, just the image of one blurred person. She pulled back her bedroom curtain an inch and scanned the area along the back alley. That's when she saw it. All the cars had been there off and on since she arrived, except one. It was a dark van with tinted windows.

Kat stepped back. Was this a coincidence? Was this someone visiting a resident in one of the other houses or had they found her? If they had found her, was Samson the reason? Had he betrayed her or was he one of them when he arrived the night before? Yet her mind couldn't accept the fact that Samson would give her away to the other side.

How was she to leave without the people in the van seeing her. She peeked through the window again. The garage across the alley. The van was parked beyond the garage and facing away from it.

When she reached the kitchen, she opened the door to the basement, and descended the steps. Sagging shelves had been built to accommo- date canned goods over a hundred years ago. She pressed a lever under third shelf then stood back as it slowly swung toward her.

There was a long passage leading under the back alley and ending at a ladder which led to the garage behind the safehouse. Once inside the garage, she stepped to the side of the window. The van was thirty feet beyond the garage. She could easily slip out unseen by the people inside the van. She opened the garage door then placed a small stone in the doorway to keep it from locking after she left.

Without looking behind her, Kat hurried down the edge of the alley. She took a roundabout path to the corner store four blocks away. Occasionally, she stopped to check a store window, but no one was following her. At least, through the haze, no one was following her that she could see.

When Kat reached her destination, she edged up to the window and peered through the corner of it. There was a customer at the counter. She waited for the customer to leave then slipped inside. She had perfected the art of a rather pathetic person in need of help, so the young man led her to the back of the store then down a short hallway where an old phone was kept. Once he returned to his duties, she tried calling Samson. No answer. She waited a few minutes then tried again. Each time Samson failed to answer, her anxiety rose just a notch.

It wasn't like him to desert her out of fear. That left two choices. He'd been captured by the people looking for her or he was one of them. If that was the case, they may be waiting for her when she returned. Then another thought struck her. Just because she didn't see anyone following her, didn't mean someone wasn't there. She was experienced at detecting someone tailing her. But they were equally experienced at not being caught doing just that.

Finally, Kat called the man she had intended to call the night before.

Chapter 6

Mr. Biggs did something Lancelot had never seen him do before. He went into the hallway and began to pace. Every twenty seconds, Lancelot saw him walking past his door with his head down and his hands clasped behind his back. After pacing for ten minutes, he walked into the decoding room, pulled on evidence gloves, and picked up the business cards the two men had left. "Taking these to the lab. Should have done it right away. Be back in a few minutes."

"Okay," Lancelot said. A moment later he jumped at the sound of Mr. Biggs' phone vibrating against the top of the desk. He answered and unconsciously put the call on speaker.

"Goliath? Goliath! Are you there?" Kat whispered as loudly as she dared.

Lancelot ran into the hallway and met Mr. Biggs coming out of the elevator. "It's Kat!"

Mr. Biggs burst through the door and grabbed the phone but, in his surprise and relief, kept the speaker phone on. "Cracker Jack? What's happening? Where are you?"

"Goliath," Kat said. "I need help."

"Where are you?" Mr. Biggs repeated. "Are you all right?"

"I'm staying at the safehouse with the tunnel under the alley?" she whispered.

"Yes! I know the one."

"I'm using the phone at that corner store four blocks away. A phone I picked up at a café last night got pitched. Someone might have traced it to me. So, he got rid of it."

Mr. Biggs' face was a study in confusion. "Who got rid of it?"

"Samson."

"Samson," Mr. Biggs murmured. "Kat, you don't' sound well. Are you all right?"

"I don't know. I can't seem to—they're looking for me, Goliath."

"Who's looking for you and why?!"

"I don't know who's looking for me. I don't know who picked me up at the airport and kept me prisoner for two days. Right now, there's a van in the alley that wasn't there before. Look, Goliath. There's been a security leak at the embassy," Kat said then hesitated. "At least I think there's been a security leak. If I'm right, it's a big one. I found out who it is then told my immediate superior. The next day I was ordered back to headquarters for a full briefing."

"Two guys posing as agents were here earlier hoping I knew where you were."

"They came to you?" Cracker Jack said. "Okay. There's something else. Samson found me at the safehouse the second night I was there, right after I returned from the café with the phone I took."

"How did Samson know you were there?"

"He said he didn't know I was there. Said his luggage got lost and all his stuff was in there. Credit cards, everything. He only had fifty dollars with him, so he came to the nearest safehouse because he didn't have enough money for a hotel."

Mr. Biggs stared at the floor. "Do you believe him?"

"Believe him? I didn't think of any reason not to believe him. We've known him for years. I just figured—I don't know anymore, Goliath."

"Okay," Mr. Biggs said. "You got the phone. Then what happened?"

"Samson arrived as soon as I got back with the phone. I explained I needed to call you. But he said we couldn't trust anybody. He said the phone could be traced, so he got rid of it. After that, we only had his phone. I wasn't sure if that was the right thing to do, but I went along with him. He left to buy supplies two hours ago and hasn't come back. It shouldn't take him more than twenty minutes." She took a deep breath. "I don't know where he is, and I'm worried something's happened to him. I just don't know what that something is."

"Do you think he deserted you?"

"I don't know," Kat said as she dropped her head and closed her eyes. "I can't believe he'd desert me but maybe he did."

"Does he still have the phone the agency issued him?"

"Yes, it's the same number so it has to be the same phone."

"You've tried to call him, right?" Mr. Biggs said.

"Yes, several times. He just isn't answering."

"Did your calls go directly to voicemail?"

"No, it didn't immediately go to voicemail" Cracker Jack said. "It rang first."

"Why isn't he answering?" Mr. Biggs murmured. "Either he ditched his phone for the same reason he got rid of yours or he's not answering it for some unfathomable reason."

"I don't know what that reason is. Right now, I need you to pick me up," Kat said, attempting to work through the fog and keep her voice low and even. "I need a safer place to stay. Farther away from here."

"All right, Kat. Don't worry. I'll develop a cover story." Mr. Biggs drew his hand across his forehead. "How did you leave the safehouse? Did the people in the van see you?"

"No, I used the tunnel."

"They didn't see you then?"

"No, the van faced in the opposite direction. And I walked in their side mirror's blind spot."

"They think you're still inside," Mr. Biggs said. "I wonder what they're waiting for. Backup maybe or nightfall."

"Yes, backup or nightfall." Should Goliath pick her up here? No, the microfilm was at the house. Why didn't she think to wear the shoes with the microfilm?

"Interesting that the van showed up after Samson left." Mr. Biggs hesitated. "They can't think I'm there to rescue you. It has to be something that's above suspicion. Except…"

"Except what?"

"Except they already know who I am."

"And those two men who came to the agency may be in the van," Kat said.

"Right. Look, we'll be there as soon as I pull something together."

"We? Who's coming with you?"

"Lancelot. He was at the safehouse the last time we were there."

"I remember Lancelot. Good choice, Goliath. He's above suspicion."

"That's what I thought. Don't worry, Kat. We'll be there soon."

"I know."

"Kat," Mr. Biggs said. "Does Samson know about those two other entrances into the house?"

"No, last night he said it was a good safehouse because there were only two entrances to worry about."

"Good, that'll help. We'll find Samson and get you situated in a new place," Mr. Biggs said. then added. "Does Sampson have a car?"

"He drove here. His car is still out front because he decided to walk. He left the keys on the kitchen table which I thought was odd."

"Just as well. We'll need it later," Mr. Biggs said. "We'll be at the safehouse as soon as we can. Okay?"

The length of Kat's sigh was very telling. "Okay. Thanks, Goliath."

Mr. Biggs' eyes focused internally with everything locked out that wasn't relevant to Kat's rescue.

Lancelot observed a side of Mr. Biggs he'd never seen before and knew nothing about. He was the most controlled man he'd ever met. Yet, at this moment, his face was contorted as he studied the phone. The boy knew the man had completely forgotten he was there. Had no idea the depth of his anxiety had an audience.

Lancelot remembered Kat. She'd only spoken to him for a few minutes, but she made a deep impression on him. And this was the same safehouse they'd used that night. "You and Kat seemed to know each other very well."

Mr. Biggs looked at him in surprise. His demeanor reverted immediately to the man Lancelot knew. "Yes, we know each other very well. She's an old friend."

"Why do you call her Cracker Jack?"

"She handled logistics when all of us were in army intelligence together and was exceptionally good at it, so we called her Cracker Jack."

"Handled logistics?"

"Right. When we were assigned a covert operation, she made sure we had all our supplies, took care of how we got there and back, was in constant contact with us to let us know if something changed that would impact our safety. That kind of thing. She never slipped up. Not once."

"And now, Kat needs help. What do you want me to do?"

"I need a few minutes to think it through," Mr. Biggs said then began to pace the hallway again.

Lancelot waited. Within minutes, he stood by his desk.

"Stand up."

"Stand up?"

"That's what I said. Stand up."

Lancelot rose then Mr. Biggs squinted as he studied him. "It might just work. About the right size, too," he muttered.

"Right size for what?"

"Tell you later." Once again, Mr. Bigg headed for the basement.

"Why hasn't Kat come to the agency looking for help?".

"She can't distinguish her friends from her enemies," he said. "Come on. We got work to do."

"What are we going to do?" Lancelot said.

"We're going to repair someone's roof."

Chapter 7

Kat remained at the back of the dark hallway until all the customers left and the young man behind the counter walked into the supply room. She'd been quietly making calls off and on for forty-five minutes. She was so quiet he'd forgotten she was there.

She walked rapidly to the edge of the front window searching for someone loitering or inside a car whose eyes were focused on the store or someone standing at a window within another shop waiting for her to leave.

Seconds later, she left the shop and turned in the opposite direction from the safehouse. She walked several blocks then changed directions twice. Each time, she stepped inside a shop stationing herself beside merchandise, but her eyes were focused on the front window. With a certain amount of confidence she wasn't being followed, she headed back to the temporary security of the safehouse.

She made her way down the alley slipping just inside backyards whenever possible. Her eyes darted side to side looking for movement of any kind, a curtain rustling, a door standing ajar, a vehicle that hadn't been there when she left.

The dark van with the tinted windows was still there. But she felt sure their eyes were focused on the backdoor. She entered the garage, made her way through the tunnel, and retraced her steps to the kitchen.

After changing into her own clothes and slipping on the shoes containing the microfilm, she entered the front bedroom and drew the curtain an inch to the side. A dark gray car was parked across the street with two men sitting inside that hadn't been there when she left.

She retrieved a pair of binoculars from her bedroom then studied the man staring at the safehouse. She didn't recognize him and she couldn't see the driver of the car.

How had they found her? Had Samson betrayed her after all? But if his intent was to betray her, why had he stayed here while they talked through various options of escape? Had he left only pretending to pick up items?

Chapter 8

"Repair someone's roof?! We don't have time for stuff like that right now. We have to figure out how we're going to rescue Kat. Anyway, I don't' know anything about repairing a roof."

"Don't have to," Mr. Biggs said as they hurried down the hall to his office. "Don't say anything while we're in here. Got that?"

"Yes. I got it."

Mr. Biggs placed the keys to his truck inside his pocket then signaled Lancelot to return to the hallway. "Do you have your phone with you?"

Lancelot carried a handheld phone device which he withdrew from his pocket.

"Let me use it for a few minutes," Mr. Biggs said then punched in a series of numbers, "Chief, got a call from Cracker Jack. She's in trouble and hiding out in that safehouse we used the last time she was here."

"Yes, I remember," Chief said. "Kat's in trouble? What kind of trouble?"

"There was a security leak at the embassy where she was assigned. She found out who it was and discussed it with someone who evidently was part of the leak. Headquarters called and said they were bringing her in for a briefing and to secure her in a safehouse."

"But the call didn't come from headquarters," Chief said.

"Right," Mr. Biggs said. "She was picked up at the airport and kept a prisoner somewhere. Kat crushed sleeping pills and put them in the guard's drink then escaped and walked to the safehouse I mentioned."

"Cracker Jack hasn't lost her touch," Chief said. "What do you want me to do?"

"Samson showed up at the safehouse then disappeared about two hours ago. I don't know what's happening there. But, I need to be able to track Samson through his phone. So I need his phone number."

"Is he still carrying an agency phone?" Chief said.

"Kat said he was and he had it when he left."

"Right. I'll check what his number is and give you a call as soon as I find out."

"There's another thing," Mr. Biggs said.

"Let's have it."

"Two men posing as officials from headquarters were here earlier. Kat hadn't called yet, so they're the ones who told me about the leak at the embassy and that she'd escaped wherever they were holding her. They wanted to know where she might go. But the print on their business cards was off. After they left, I called Ed at human resources and he never heard of them. I asked him about Kat and he said she was still at the embassy where she'd been assigned. So headquarters doesn't know she's missing. Somebody at the embassy is covering for her disappearance. I took their cards to the lab. They're checking for fingerprints."

"The security leak must be very serious if they're going to this extend to find her."

"Right, they're worried we'll get to her before they do and reveal who's leaking the information," Mr. Biggs said.

"I agree," Chief said.

"Look, Chief, I need to know if they've stationed people outside the agency to follow me when I leave here. I'm going to do a little test run to check it out. If somebody tails me, I'll need a decoy posing as me to drive my truck. I'll leave my phone, truck keys, coat, and hat on my desk for the person who takes my place. Don't know who that might be yet, but I'll call Bake. He's good at figuring out stuff like that. No one will suspect the kid's going with me, so you can contact me through him. I'm using his phone right now so you'll have his number for reference. If I'm being followed, I'll use the van and you can call me on the phone we leave in there."

Good idea, Goliath," Chief said. "Bake is good at logistics."

"I want backup near the safehouse but out of sight until we need them. And we should fly Kat out of the area to a more secure safehouse."

"I'll take care of both," Chief said.

After Mr. Biggs disconnected his call, they hurried down the hallway and out the backdoor where the old, rusted-out truck was located in an enclosed parking lot. Once they were settled in their seats, he said, "Okay, kid. I need you to punch in a few numbers into your contact list. Mr. Biggs gave Lancelot the numbers then pulled out of the parking lot driving at a leisurely pace while Lancelot fixed his eyes on the side mirror.

Within a few seconds, Lancelot spotted a car pull out from a parking space and follow them at a distance. "There's a car back there."

"I saw it, too. Let's drive another block and see what happens when I make a turn."

Lancelot continued to keep the car behind them in view. The driver kept a half block space between them appearing to be heading in the same direction. Yet, when Mr. Biggs turned, the car followed. Three blocks later, the security guard turned in another direction. The car executed the same turn.

"Okay, now we know," Mr. Biggs said. "Bake was the first number I gave you. Call him."

"Mr. Baker? Your old army buddy?"

"Yes. Get him on your phone. Put it on speaker so I can talk to him."

When someone answered, Lancelot said. "Mr. Baker? Mr. Biggs wants to talk to you."

"Bake?" Mr. Biggs said. "Look, got a problem. It's about Cracker Jack."

"Something's wrong with Kat?" Mr. Baker said, his voice filled with concern.

"Two guys posing as officials from headquarters stopped by today hoping I knew where she was."

"Is she in danger?" Mr. Baker said.

"Yes. Don't know how bad it is, but I'll let you know."

"Do you know who those guys are?"

"No, the lab is checking their fingerprints. Don't know how many people are involved in tracking her down. Need two things from you and the boys, Bake."

"Whatever you need, Goliath."

"I need a decoy, somebody who looks enough like me to come through the alley and enter the backdoor of the agency. He'll put on my hat and coat, leave in my truck, and go to my place. He needs to take my phone in case they use it to track me."

There was silence for a moment. "Charlie. I'll get Charlie. Same height and build."

"Charlie's perfect. Thanks, Bake," Mr. Biggs said. "They were stupid enough to bug my office. I don't want to remove it yet."

"Okay, I'll tell him. What else do you need?"

"Kat's at the safehouse we used when she was here the last time. I need you and a couple of the boys to wait nearby in case I need you. Chief is sending backup, too, but they need to be positioned farther away. You and the boys won't arouse suspicion."

"Will do, Biggs," Mr. Baker said. "If there's anything else we can do, let me know."

"Thanks, Bake. One more thing. Sampson was with her. He went out to get supplies this morning and didn't return.

"Samson? He'd never leave her by choice. They must have him unless…"

"I know. I thought of that, too." Mr. Biggs said in a tight voice. "No idea where he might be. As soon as Chief calls me with his phone number, we'll use it to find him."

As soon as the call was ended, Lancelot said, "Who's Samson?"

"Samson was an important member of our army intelligence team. It's hard for me to believe he'd betray us."

Chapter 9

Mr. Biggs headed back to the agency, parked his truck, then hurried down the hall to his office with Lancelot close behind. "Stay quiet," he reminded the young decoder.

Inside his office, Mr. Biggs searched through his closet finally selecting two jackets and two caps. The labels read "Heating and Plumbing". He ripped off the labels and replaced them with "Roofing and Siding".

Tossing the smaller jacket and cap to Lancelot, he stuffed a set of keys inside his pocket then trotted down the hallway to the basement.

"What are you getting?" Lancelot said, clambering down the steps to keep up with him.

"A tracking device. If Samson's still carrying his phone, that's the only way we'll be able to locate him." Mr. Biggs carried it up the stairs and the two trotted out the backdoor.

The small garage was situated at the very end of the lot. Currently, the sides of the van were blank. Mr. Biggs unlocked the driver's side and placed the tracking instrument on the floor. Stepping to the end of the van, he chose two large signs that read, "Roofing and Siding". He gave one of the signs to Lancelot. "Put that one on your side," he said. "Make sure it's centered and level. Someone will spot it in a second if it's crooked."

"Right." Lancelot hung the sign, adjusted it twice before it was perfect.

Mr. Biggs slid behind the wheel of the van and backed out of the garage. But instead of heading to the usual exit, he drove to a wall directly opposite the exit.

"You're going the wrong way," Lancelot said.

"There are people outside the regular exit. We just saw them. They're not stupid. They know we conducted a test run to see if we were being followed."

"I get it. Now, they're waiting for some kind of disguise. Right?"

"Right, and that's the problem. They'd spot the van and follow us. Even if they don't follow us, they'll call someone and give them a description of the van so their accomplices will be on the lookout for us." Mr. Biggs said. "Three people in the entire agency know what you're about to see. I trust you or you wouldn't be that fourth person. Do you understand?"

"I understand."

Mr. Biggs reached under his seat and pressed a button.. A part of the wall moved aside and they drove through it. Lancelot peered into his side mirror and the wall automatically slid back as if it had never moved. "Wow," he murmured softly.

They drove down an alley with high walls on both sides until they reached another wall. Mr. Biggs pressed a second button and the wall slid to the side allowing them to drive through.

At the end of the lane, there was a wrought iron gate that automatically opened when they came near. Mr. Biggs eased onto the street then made several turns constantly checking his rearview mirror. In fifteen minutes, Mr. Biggs nodded to the right. "See the corner store?"

"Yes, I see it."

"The corner store is four blocks from the safehouse. Cracker Jack used the phone in there to make her calls. Just remember where the corner store is relative to the safehouse."

At some point, Lancelot would be on his own but for how long and what would he be expected to do? It's the unknown that is unsettling. "Okay, I'll remember where the corner store is."

As he drove the last four blocks, Mr. Biggs searched the area. "There," he said, looking at a dark gray car parked a block away.

"That car? Is it important?"

"That car looks very different from the other cars along this street. I suspect the two men who visited our office this morning are sitting inside keeping watch over the safehouse."

There was another car parked across the street. "How about that car?" Lancelot said.

Mr. Biggs was still focused on the dark gray car with his brows drawn together. So Lancelot turned his head wondering what it was about that car that worried him. He repeated the question. "How about that car sitting across the street?"

Mr. Biggs pulled his attention away from the dark gray car. "That's Samson's car. He parked it in front of the safehouse."

Lancelot counted the houses to the end of the street. "The safehouse is the fourth one from the end And Kat's in there waiting for us."

"Yes," Mr. Biggs said vaguely.

"Do you think the people in that dark gray are watching us?"

"They're watching us, all right." Mr. Biggs drove to the end of the street, turned right then pulled down an alley behind the houses. Ahead of them was a van parked close to the edge to allow traffic to go through. Its windows were deeply tinted so it was impossible to see if anyone was inside.

"Are they related to that car across the street from the safehouse?"

Mr. Biggs chuckled. "They're related."

"How are we going to get into the safehouse? They've got the front and back covered?"

"There's a way we use only in emergencies." Mr. Biggs said. "It's three houses down. We walk up to the attic then go over the roof on our hands and knees."

Lancelot swallowed and peered at the roof line. "It's a long way down."

Mr. Biggs glanced at the boy. "The key is not to fall."

"Right." Lancelot continued to study the rooftop. "We don't want anyone seeing us actually entering her house. But, it's three floors up there and three floors to the ground if we fall."

"We won't fall."

"Here's hoping," Lancelot murmured then he connected the dots.

"That's why we're Roofing and Siding so if someone does see us up there, they'll think we're working on a roofing problem."

"That's the idea, kid."

As Mr. Biggs parked the van, a phone rang under the driver's seat. He reached under his seat, disconnected the phone from its charger, and answered it. "Good. Samson's phone number. Hopefully, he's still got it with him and I can track where he is. After we get Kat out of the safehouse, I'll work on it. Thanks, Chief," he said then replaced the phone and turned to Lancelot. "Pull your hat down and keep your head lowered until we get through the door." He grabbed two tool boxes from the back, giving one to Lancelot.

First, they heard the sound of the minivan window being lowered. A few seconds later, they heard the door open.

Chapter 10

Mr. Biggs sensed Lancelot was about to turn his head. "Don't look, kid. Just keep moving."

Although, he desperately wanted to see what danger lurked behind him, Lancelot forced himself to focus ahead. "What if they get out and come towards us?"

Mr. Biggs got behind Lancelot and placed a steady hand on the boy's back pressing him forward. "Right now, they don't know who we are. They're not as suspicious as they are curious. Just relax and don't hurry. We'll be inside in a few seconds."

They slowly walked up the sidewalk like two tired workmen going to their next job. Mr. Biggs knocked soundly on the door. "Stand behind me and to the side. Don't want them to see I'm using a key to get in." Once the door was unlocked, Mr. Biggs spoke in a voice that carried down the street. "Having trouble with a leak on the roof? Okay. We'll take a look at it and see what needs to be done."

They slid into the kitchen then locked the door behind them. Lancelot melted against the wall and closed his eyes. As difficult as that was, the worst was yet to come.

Mr. Biggs placed his tool kit on the floor then pried Lancelot's tool kit out of his hand setting it down beside his own. He studied the boy then gave him a minute to recover. "Ready?"

Lancelot shoved himself away from the wall, then followed Mr. Biggs down the hallway and up the steps two-at-a-time. When they reached the attic, there was a ladder leading to the roof.

"We'll stand up, look around, and drop down so they can't see us. Then we'll move three houses down where Kat is hiding. Got that?"

"I think so."

"Just watch me and do whatever I do. Okay?"

"Right. Do whatever you do."

"Do not look down." Mr. Biggs climbed the ladder then searched the area for the nonexistent leaking problem.

When Lancelot joined the head of security on the roof, his eyes drifted over the surface duplicating Mr. Biggs' movements.

Mr. Biggs pointed to a spot then knelt as if to examine it more closely. Lancelot dropped down beside him. At this level, they were out of sight to anyone on the ground. He crawled along after Mr. Biggs over several more roofs until they reached the safehouse.

Mr. Biggs slipped his finger inside a metal ring invisible unless someone knew it was there. It was dark inside and Lancelot wasn't all that crazy about dropping into what looked like a black abyss waiting to swallow him up.

Mr. Biggs made his way slowly down the ladder into the attic followed close behind by the decoder. When his head cleared the roofline, Mr. Biggs said in a low voice, "Reach up and pull the door down after you."

Lancelot drew the door shut, found his way down the ladder, and stood beside Mr. Biggs.

Mr. Biggs grasped the boy's arm, led him across the floor, and opened the attic door. When dim light flooded in, they made their way down a short hallway to the steps leading to the second floor of the townhouse.

Kat was waiting for them and breathed a sigh of relief then stretched out her arms to Mr. Biggs. "Goliath," she whispered.

Lancelot leaned his back against the wall while they hugged. He'd never seen the head of security touch anyone except to give his old army buddies a slap on the back or help him through a crisis.

When they broke apart, Kat said, "Did you have any trouble?"

"No, we made a trial run out of the agency parking lot using my truck."

"You were followed?"

"Right, they weren't shy about letting us know they were following us either."

"How did you get here?" Kat said.

"We used the van. Roofing and Siding this time. When we got out of the van, the guys parked in the alley looked at us. Even opened their door, but decided we were nothing to worry about. I hope that feeling lasts until we get you out of here," Mr. Biggs said.

"You saw the lookout in the alley. Did you see the car across the street?" Kat said.

"We saw it," Mr. Biggs said. "How long have they been here?"

"The car across the street was here when I returned from contacting you. The van was here before I left," Kat said, drawing in a deep breath. "I know you have a plan worked out or you wouldn't be here."

"We need to stay here as long as it would take to check out a leaky roof three houses down."

Kat nodded. They'd used that cover story before.

Mr. Biggs turned to Lancelot whose gaze was directed at the floor. "You remember Lancelot Maddox."

"Of course I remember Lancelot," Kat said. In spite of the overriding tension, she smiled and gave him a quick hug.

For his entire life, Lancelot had discouraged hugs from anyone except his mother. But this was someone different. He found himself hugging her in return.

Kat stepped back and turned her attention to Mr. Biggs. "Okay, tell me what you've got."

"The kid is about your size. You can wear his jacket and hat. Are there any slacks about the same color as his in the closet?"

"Very close," Kat said. She studied Lancelot then nodded. "You're right. We're about the same size. Should work. I'll put them on when we're ready to leave."

Lancelot's head shot up now. If Cracker Jack was going to pretend to be him, just how was he going to get out of here?

"What happens to Lancelot after we leave?" Kat said.

"He'll stay here ten minutes. That'll give us time to crawl over the roof and drive away. We'll wait at the corner store where you called us. I have the tracker with me, and Chief gave me Samson's number, so while we're waiting we'll look for him."

"I still can't believe he would betray us," Kat said softly. "So, Lancelot will use Samson's car as a decoy."

"Right," Mr. Biggs said.

Lancelot kept his head lowered. He didn't want them to see the rising panic he felt. If Mr. Biggs had known about this plan all along, why did he wait until now to spring it on him?

Kat took a closer look at the young decoder. "He doesn't look old enough to drive."

Lancelot shifted positions so his body faced them but continued to stare at the floor. He was one of those nerdy kids who preferred sitting in front of a computer rather than behind the wheel of a car.

"Fourteen," Mr. Biggs said. "Plenty old enough to do this job. Anyway, he's a very capable kid."

The compliment eased some of the fear of having his life, and possibly his death, sketched out for him. He straightened his shoulders and stood just a little taller. Yet, there was something he absolutely had to explain to them.

"Lancelot, do you think you can do this?" Kat said softly.

The longer Kat held Lancelot's gaze, the more determined he became to live up to her expectations and the more he forgot the important information he absolutely had to explain. "Yes. I'm sure I can," he said.

Kat nodded her approval. "Good." She drew in her breath then opened a door. "I'll change now. There's a jacket and hat I wore when I came here," she said. "They'll know what I was wearing, so he'll need to have those on when he leaves." She turned to Lancelot. "Do you mind wearing them when you leave?"

At the moment, wearing a women's jacket and hat made no difference whatsoever to Lancelot. "No, I don't mind at all."

"You're a fine young man, Lancelot," Kat said, giving him another quick hug.

Suddenly, Lancelot completely understood why everyone rushed in to save this woman.

"I'll slip into my other pair of slacks and be out in a minute."

While Kat was in the room changing, Mr. Biggs turned to Lancelot. "Look, kid. You saw that dark gray car out front, right?

"Right."

"And you remember where the corner store is, right?"

"Right," Lancelot said, trying to maintain a confident look, but he was beginning to lose some of the enthusiasm he had while staring into Kat's eyes. Now, his hands and forehead were growing damp.

"Okay, this is what I want you to do. Ten minutes after we leave, I want you to put on Kat's jacket and zip it up as far as it will go. Pull up the collar, pull down the hat, and keep you hands in your pockets when you walk to Samson's car. And, whatever you do, keep your head down so all they see is the top of your hat. Don't rush it but move as quickly as you can without looking as though you're in a raging hurry. Okay."

"Okay."

"Now, this is the tough part," Mr. Biggs said, actually placing his hand on Lancelot's shoulder, which was a very bad sign. "Those guys are going to follow you, so you've got to lose them. The only way you can do that is to time it so you run through a red light and they'll be stuck at the light." He looked at the boy who, by now, was nodding his head absently while swallowing at the same time.

"This is the best method to do it if you can manage it. Are you listening?

"I'm l-listening," Lancelot stammered, trying to remember what it was he desperately needed to explain.

"When you look ahead and see a light is about to change, pass the car in front of you then charge through the red light. That way, there's a car between you and the car following you. It will have to stop at the red light to avoid hitting the car you just passed. Got that?"

"I get it but what if it's a no-passing zone?"

"Look, kid," Mr. Biggs said, shifting his weight. "In this business, we can't worry about no-passing zones, red lights, or one-way streets. We're here to do a job and that's what we're going to do. Got it?"

Slowly, Lancelot nodded his head.

Kat walked out wearing a different pair of slacks. After they exchanged jackets and hats, she gathered her hair then slowly drew her hair inside the Roofing and Siding hat. "How's that look?" she asked Goliath. "All my hair tucked in?"

Mr. Biggs inspected her hair for any trailing bits then nodded.

Kat handed Lancelot the key to Samson's car and said, "We'd better practice the walk. Lancelot, I want you to try to mimic how I walk and move." When Lancelot nodded, she walked up and down the hallway several times.

Lancelot studied Kat's walk then, after several attempts, he was able to imitate her enough not to arouse suspicion with the people in the dark gray car across the street.

Mr. Biggs and Kat drew in their collective breaths as they stood side-by-side studying Lancelot who studied the floor.

"Do you think you can do this, Lancelot?" Kat said. Her expression allowed for a backdoor escape if he needed it.

If he didn't go through with it, Lancelot would forever feel like a failure in his own eyes and probably their eyes as well. Although, they'd never openly blame him. He lifted his chin and said with far more confidence than he felt, "Sure. I can do it."

Goliath and Cracker Jack exchanged knowing looks. They'd been in tighter spots than this dozens of times. The difficult could be accomplished; the impossible just took a little longer. And, because of Lancelot's inexperience, this might take even longer still.

"Check your watch, kid, then wait ten minutes," Mr. Biggs said.

"Okay" Lancelot held his wrist tightly with the other hand so they wouldn't see it shake as he checked the time.

Mr. Biggs slapped him on the back, but Kat gave him a hug then they climbed the steps to the attic and Lancelot was left alone.

Chapter 11

Lancelot walked down the stairs to the ground floor and sat on the bottom step. He willed his watch to slow down but it ignored him and raced around in circles until the ten minutes were nearly gone. He opened the door then completely forgot how to walk. He pulled the hat down as far as it would go, dropped his chin, stuffed his hands inside his pockets. and moved towards the car. The car unlocked as soon as he neared it and he slid behind the wheel.

Suddenly, he remembered what he desperately needed to tell them. Mr. Biggs' truck was old. He'd sat beside him in the truck many times and knew exactly how it worked.

His parents owned a fairly new van. His two older brothers always sat in the two seats behind the front seats, so he sat way in the back where he couldn't see anything the driver did. To add to that, he had a shocking lack of curiosity about automobiles. His two brothers loved cars and got their driver's license as soon as possible. He had little interest in getting his license.

Lancelot didn't know how they started the car or where anything was, like the turn signal or the windshield wipers or the headlights. Sweat formed around the rim of his hat and trickled down his face. He rubbed his damp hands together as his eyes stared blankly at the overwhelming information that lay before him. Well, it couldn't be that hard. People did this every day.

Lancelot resisted the temptation to glance at the dark gray car across the street. Instead, he looked at the confusing buttons scattered all over the place. He spotted a likely suspect and pressed on it gently. He closed his eyes when the engine turned over and began to hum.

Now, what? He knew the car had to be in drive mode in order to move forward. Within seconds, he figured that out, too. He pressed down too hard on the accelerator and shot forward. He took his foot off the pedal then pressed down again, more gently this time, but was still off to a rather impressive start.

Within half a block, the enemy car was behind him. The van he'd seen parked in the alley pulled onto the main street and fell behind the dark gray car. Both were following him at a close distance. They were practically on his tail but there was nothing he could do except keep moving until he got to a light that was about to change. Driving in a straight line wasn't too tough. Passing a car and turning a corner at a high rate of speed would be another story. Except, there was no car ahead of him to pass.

One block later, a car pulled out from a side street. Lancelot hadn't so much as turned a corner, yet now he had to pass his gigantic car ahead of him, whip through a red light, and make a rapid right-hand turn then another then another until he was sure he'd lost those guys who doggedly tailed him.

Finally, his opportunity presented itself. There was a green light ahead that was sure to change any second. He shoved down on the accelerator and nearly crashed into the car ahead until he turned the steering wheel to pass it. Unfortunately, he turned the steering wheel too far and created a rather memorable dent in a parked car two lanes over. Who knows what the fender of Samson's car looked like?

Lancelot over corrected again and missed the car he was trying to pass by inches only because the driver squealed his tires as he applied the brakes.

The light was turning yellow then red as Lancelot reached the intersection. He barreled through it while everyone behind came to a screeching halt. He made a somewhat successful turn, only putting a slight crease in another unsuspecting parked car. He made a quick left-hand turn then a right only running over the curb once, but at least he avoided mutilating another car. His eyes darted back and forth. Where was he and how was he to ever find that corner store?

Lancelot crushed down the rising panic and turned right at the next intersection where he fought the next battle. He'd turned onto a one-way street where two solid lanes of traffic were currently bearing down on him at an astronomical speed. He caught his breath and fought down that state of fear that causes the mind to cease functioning. He edged over to the curb where his front, right tire popped onto the sidewalk then waited for the onslaught to pass.

While he waited, he placed his head on the steering wheel. Hopeless. He was completely untrained and unprepared for this entire mission which, at the moment. was begging for failure. Why hadn't Mr. Baker or someone else been asked to do this? He knew why. They were too big. They never would have passed for Kat.

His peripheral vision assured him that the coast was clear. Cautiously, he pulled off the curb which created a rather interesting bounce and scratching sound as the front end caught the cement sidewalk. He was doing the best he could, which wasn't saying much.

The worst was yet to come. Lancelot made a quick left-hand turn and found himself on a dead-end street. He'd forgotten to check for the dark gray car and the van following it. He glanced at the rearview mirror and there they were closing in. How did they find him so quickly? Panic set in as he searched for a way out. There had to be an alley. But there wasn't one and the two vehicles were nearly on his tail.

Chapter 12

Lancelot reached the end of the one-way street and was forced to stop. He stared in horror as the two vehicles pulled up thirty feet behind him and three men got out and approached his car from the rear. He'd seen two of them at the agency earlier that day.

A brilliant, if temporary, solution struck him and he threw the car into reverse. By now, he had plenty of practice in shoving down on the accelerator and he brought that to bear. The three men scattered as the car shot past them crashing into the dark gray car. The hood buckled and steam rolled out of the broken radiator. That car was toast.

Having recovered from the shock of being nearly killed, the three men approached the car cautiously from the side. Lancelot may not be a seasoned agent, but this strategy seemed to be working, so he threw the car into drive and shoved down on the accelerator moving forty feet ahead.

The three men had an opportunity to see his face and knew they'd been setup. Drawing guns out of their shoulder holsters, they marched forward. At the same time, the van behind the wrecked car worked its way around the disabled dark gray car and moved ahead hoping to trap Lancelot at the end of the one-way street.

Lancelot viewed the men with the guns in his rearview mirror. Fear is a powerful force but so is adrenaline. It worked once, so Lancelot tried it again. As the van approached, he shoved the car into reverse and the two vehicles collided.

Lancelot wore his seatbelt; they did not and their heads hit the windshield. The three men with the guns were his final test and he had no idea how to conquer them. Fearful of being runover, they split up and headed for the sidewalks on both sides of the street.

It's one thing to hit a car but quite another to hit a human being. Lancelot couldn't do that so he braced himself for the worst.

But the worst didn't happen. First, the Roofing and Siding van showed up followed by two other cars. Six men flew out of the two cars and quickly corralled the three men on the sidewalk.

An ambulance roared around the corner and took control of the men with head injuries. Within ten minutes, they left for the hospital with an unmarked car following close behind.

Lancelot's adrenaline had plummeted and he laid his head back. It was over. His job was done. His car door opened and Mr. Biggs squatted down and touched his arm.

"Kid? You okay?" When Lancelot turned his head and nodded, Mr. Biggs helped him out of the car and half carried him to the Roofing and Siding van where Kat waited for him.

"Should we take him to the hospital?" Kat said.

"No, I don't want to go to the hospital. I'm okay."

Mr. Biggs and Kat studied the young man who was exhausted but seemed physically unharmed. "Airport," Mr. Biggs said and they piled into the van.

Lancelot reclined behind the two front seats while Mr. Biggs headed for the small airport the agency used. "Does Kat need to leave since they were arrested?"

"Don't know if we got everybody," Mr. Biggs said. "Can't take the chance."

"So many people showed up to rescue me. What happened?"

"When we drove past the safehouse, we saw that dark gray car parked across the street. Do you remember that?" Mr. Biggs said looking at Lancelot in his rearview mirror.

"I remember. You had an odd look on your face."

"Right. Well, I saw someone in the backseat sit up then lay down again. Didn't feel right. When Kat and I left you in the safehouse and drove out of the alley, I gave her Samson's phone number and she tracked it to that dark gray car. That's when we knew where he was."

"He was a traitor," Lancelot said softly. "But why did he do it? And how did he know Kat was at that safehouse?"

"Kat had a lot of old friends in army intelligence," Mr. Biggs said. "They must have discovered Samson was taking a flight here, waited for him at the airport then offered him enough money that he changed sides. Samson probably knew Kat would head for a safehouse."

"I doubt if he knew I was in that safehouse until he walked through the door," Kat said.

It's devastating when someone you trust turns against you so the three of them were silent until they reached the airport.

Twenty minutes later, they pulled down a narrow lane leading to a small hangar. A four-seater plane awaited them.

Three people stood beside the plane waiting to take Kat to a safe-house where security would watch over her.

Kat placed her hands on Lancelot's shoulders and kissed his check. "You're an amazing, resourceful young man."

Lancelot attempted to control the grin that was begging to break out on his face. "Oh, it wasn't much," he finally said.

When the pilot approached Mr. Biggs said, "Plane ready?"

"Yes, sir. Already filed a flight plan, so we're ready to go."

"Good. You'd better get going then," Mr. Biggs said. He turned to Kat then looked away before turning back. "You're safe and you've got the microfilm."

Kat nodded and stood for a moment equally reluctant to leave. But there was urgency to get her to safety, so she hugged the two who were responsible for rescuing her then followed the pilot to the plane.

Mr. Biggs pressed the edge of his hand above his eyes and watched the plane roll down the runway and take off. When the plane flew above the clouds, he drew his lips inside his mouth then returned to the van. His face was drawn and he was silent for a few minutes then turned to Lancelot. "You sure you're okay?"

"I'm sure," Lancelot said even though he'd never felt so exhausted in his life.

"Great job, kid. Couldn't have done better myself."

That was rare praise and, exhausted as Lancelot was, he responded with a weak smile.

Mr. Biggs didn't hum and tap out a tune on the steering wheel as he always did. This was different and they drove back to the agency in silence.

~The End~